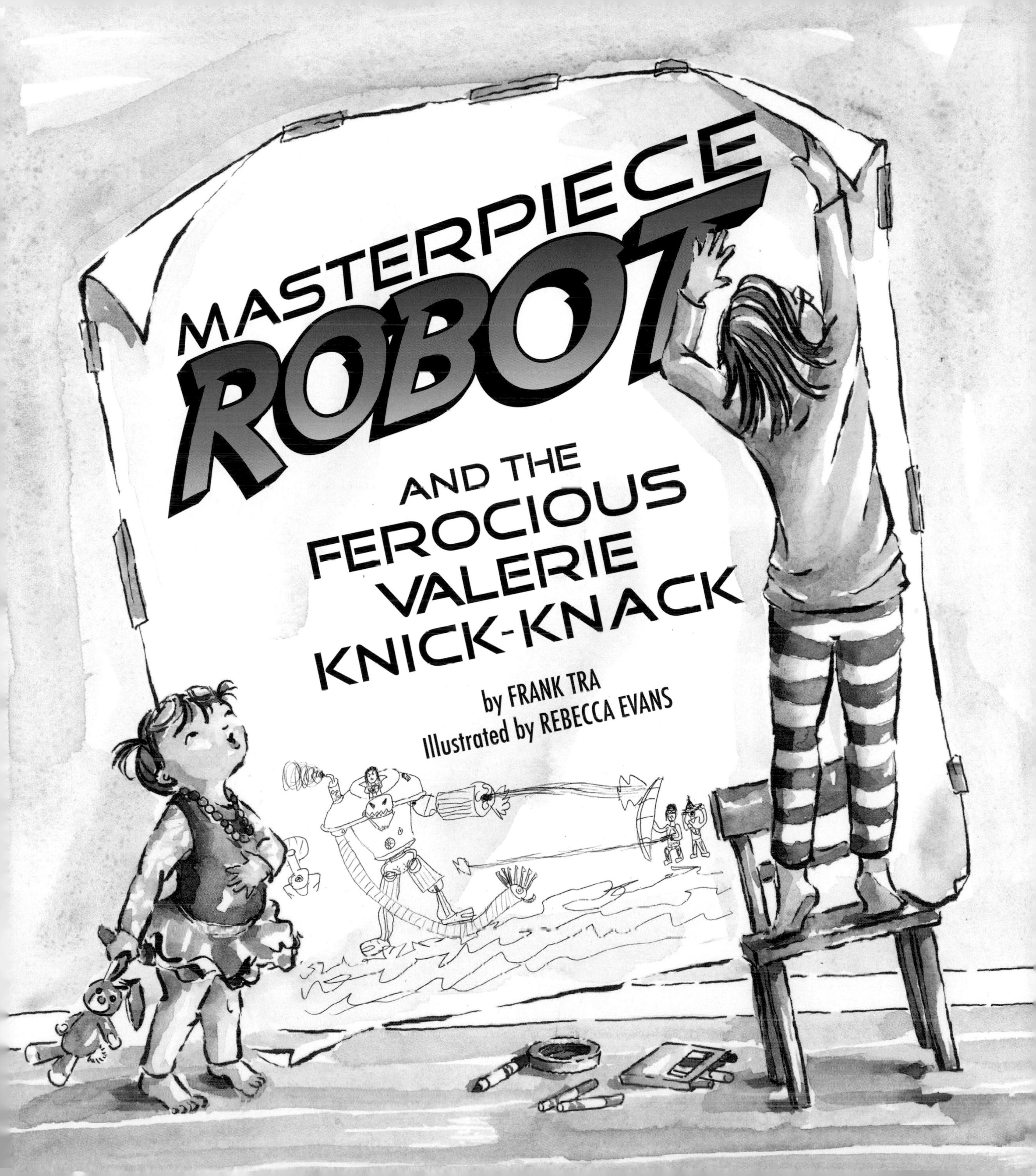

MASTERPIECE ROBOT

AND THE FEROCIOUS VALERIE KNICK-KNACK

by FRANK TRA
Illustrated by REBECCA EVANS

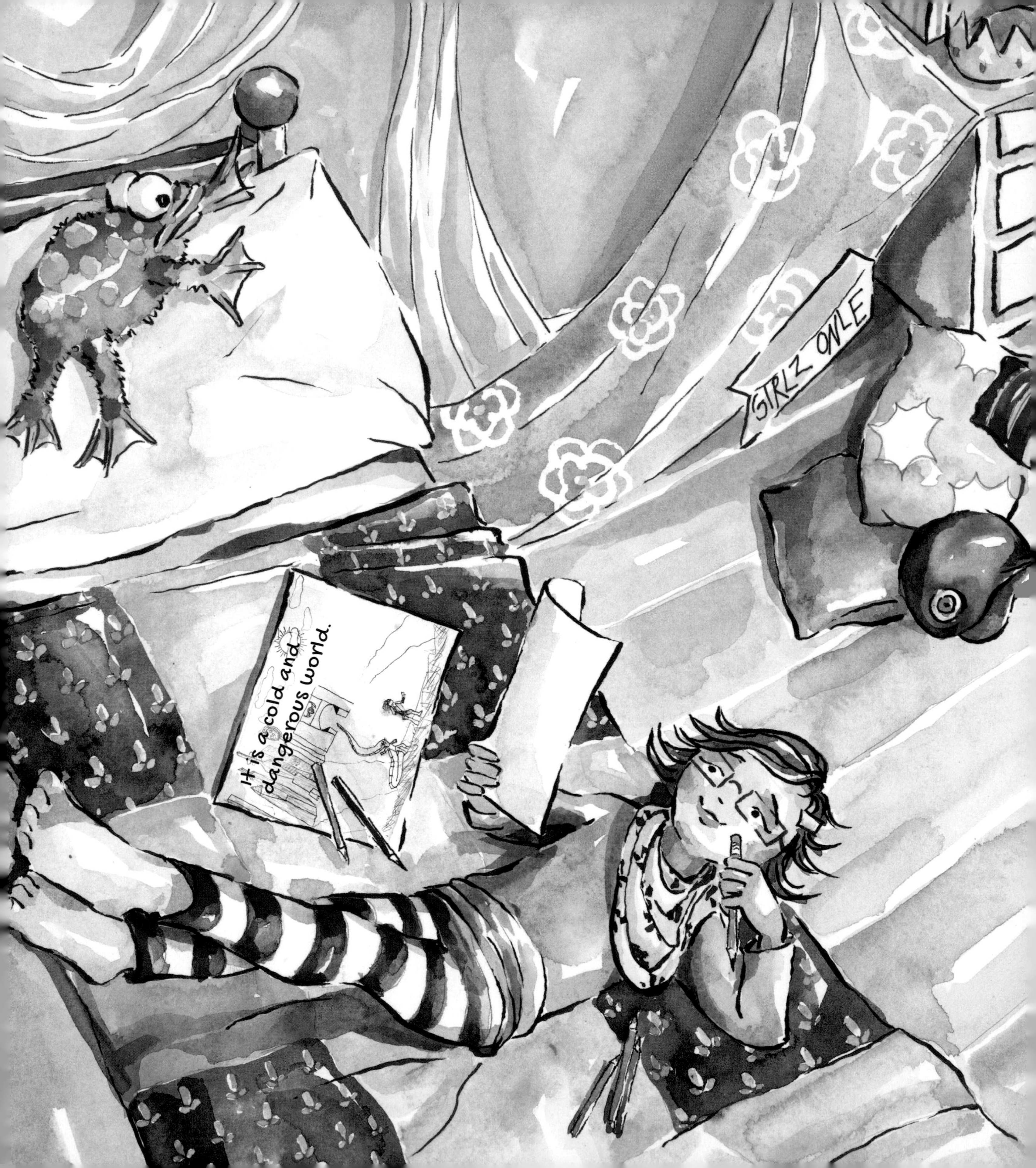
GIRLZ ONLE
It is a cold and dangerous world.

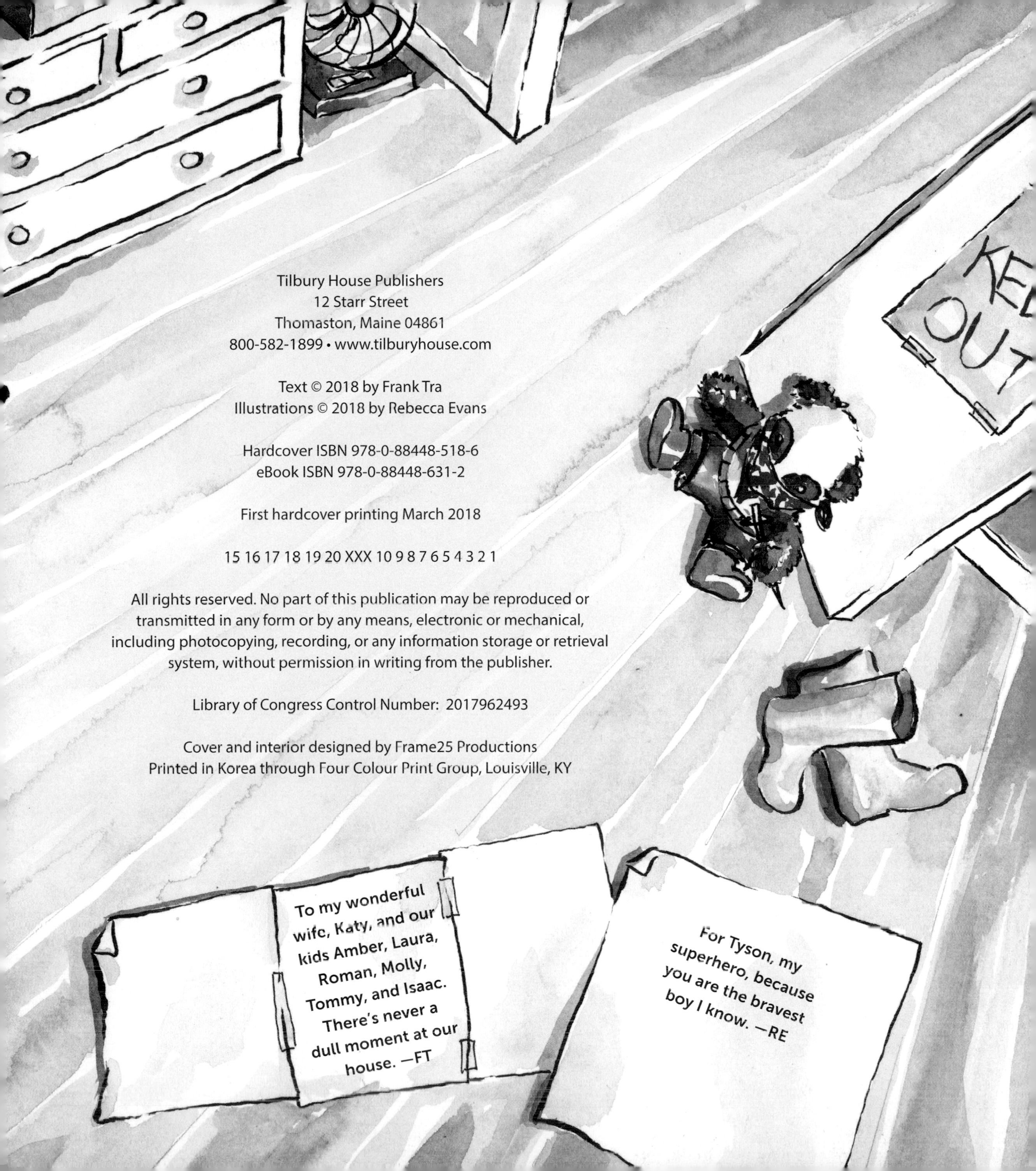

Tilbury House Publishers
12 Starr Street
Thomaston, Maine 04861
800-582-1899 • www.tilburyhouse.com

Hardcover ISBN 978-0-88448-518-6
eBook ISBN 978-0-88448-631-2

First hardcover printing March 2018

15 16 17 18 19 20 XXX 10 9 8 7 6 5 4 3 2 1

Library of Congress Control Number: 2017962493

Cover and interior designed by Frame25 Productions
Printed in Korea through Four Colour Print Group, Louisville, KY

To my wonderful wife, Katy, and our kids Amber, Laura, Roman, Molly, Tommy, and Isaac. There's never a dull moment at our house. —FT

For Tyson, my superhero, because you are the bravest boy I know. —RE

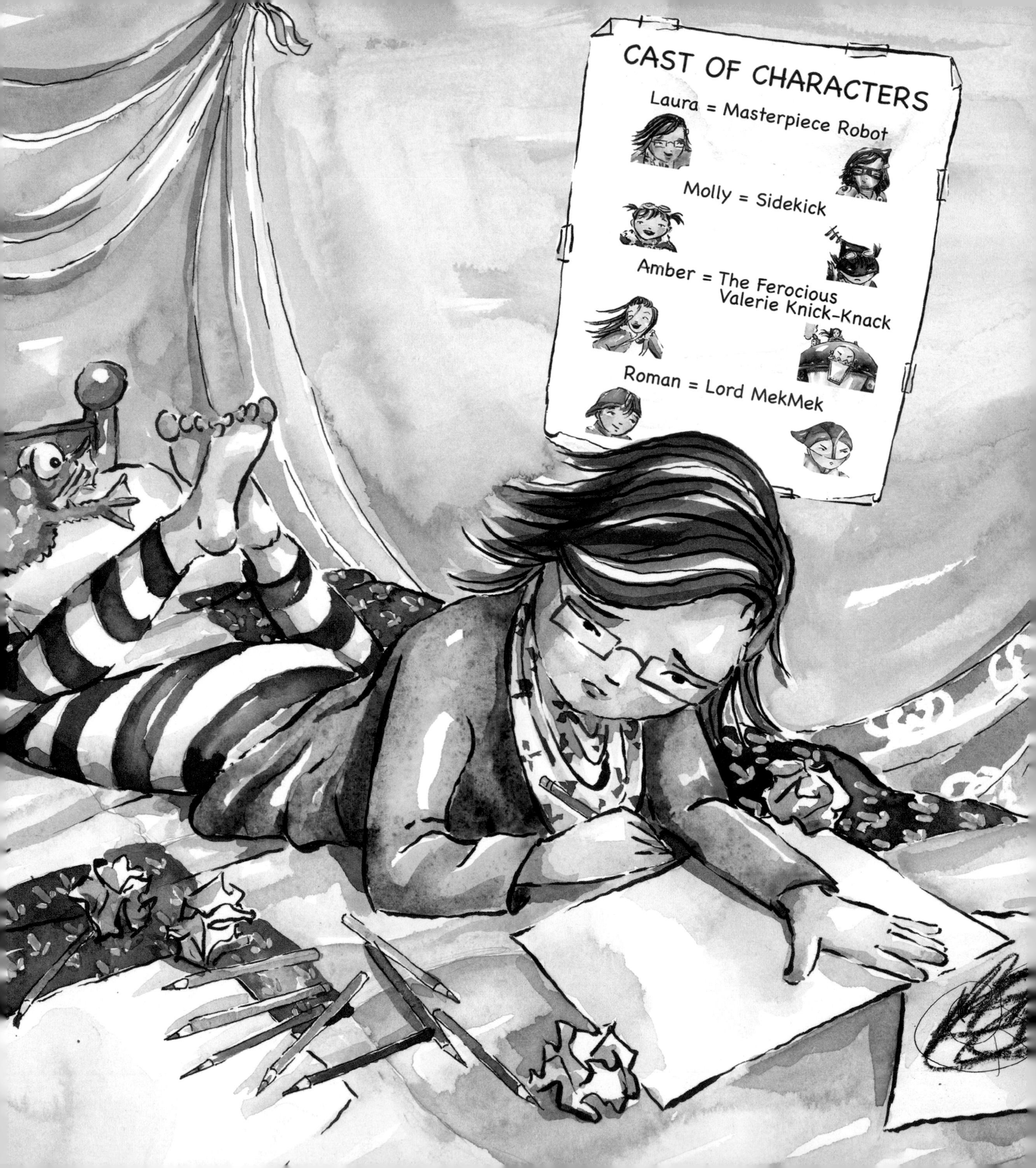
CAST OF CHARACTERS
Laura = Masterpiece Robot
Molly = Sidekick
Amber = The Ferocious Valerie Knick-Knack
Roman = Lord MekMek

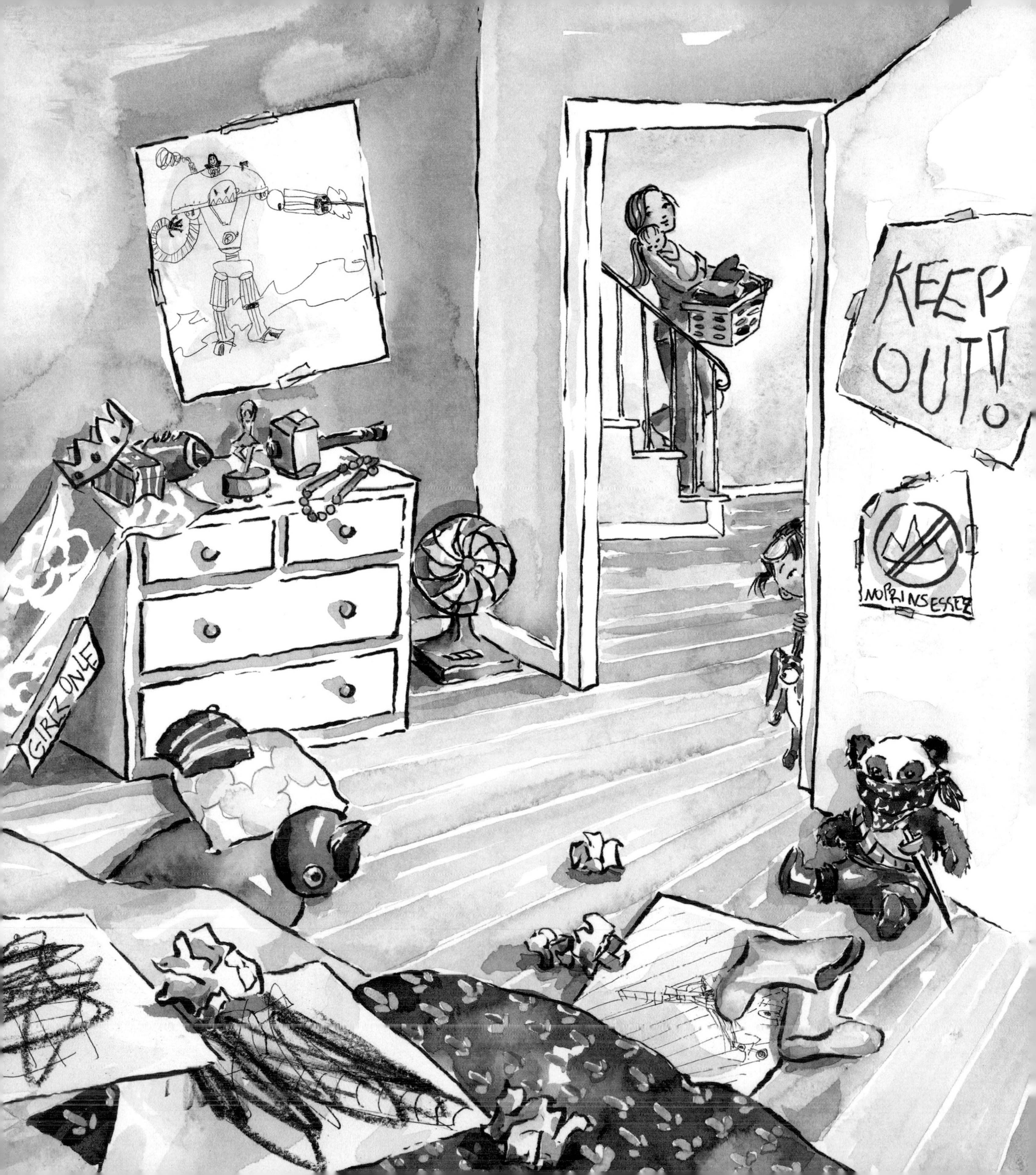
KEEP OUT!
NO PRINSESSEZ

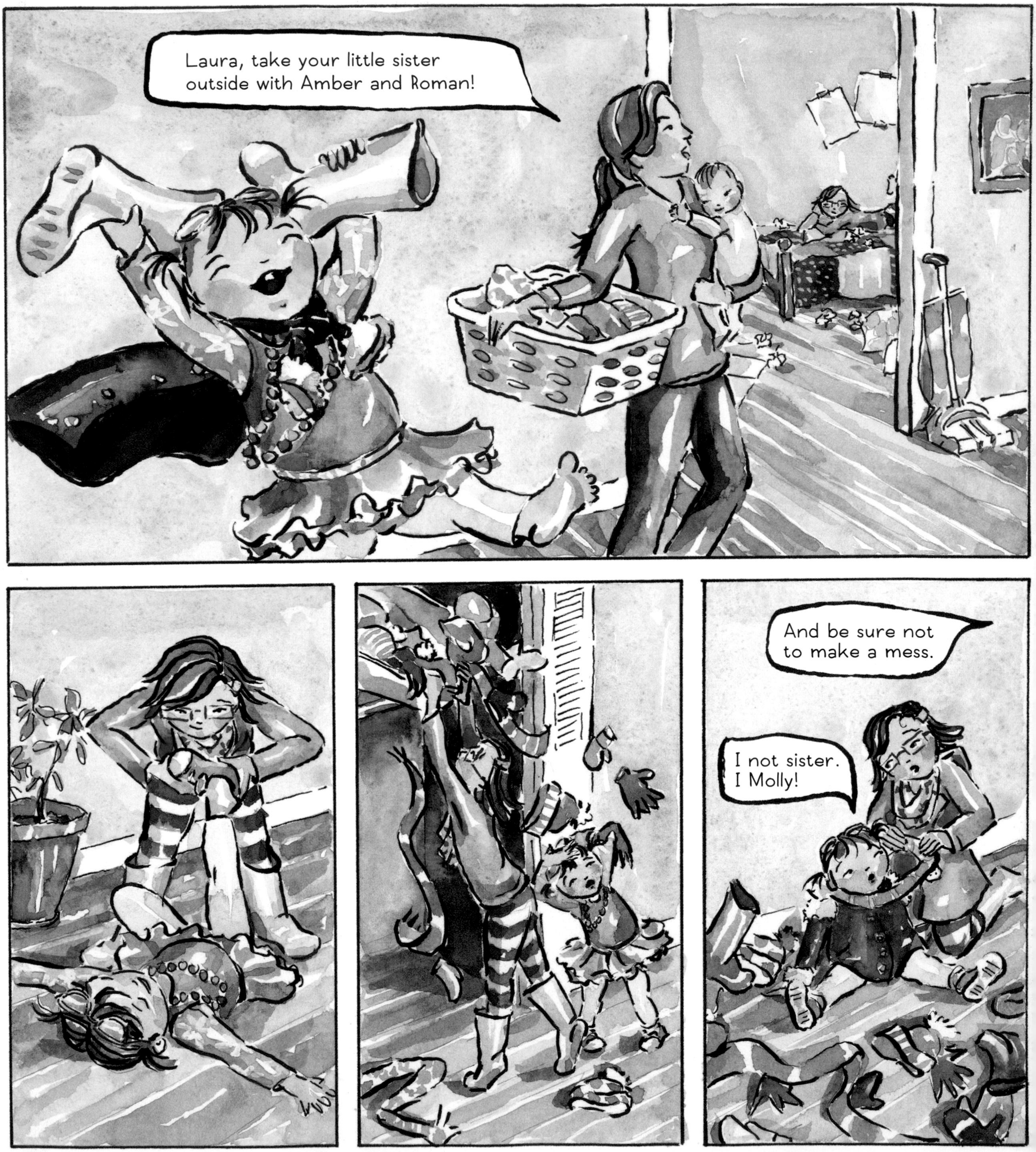
Laura, take your little sister outside with Amber and Roman!
And be sure not to make a mess.
I not sister. I Molly!

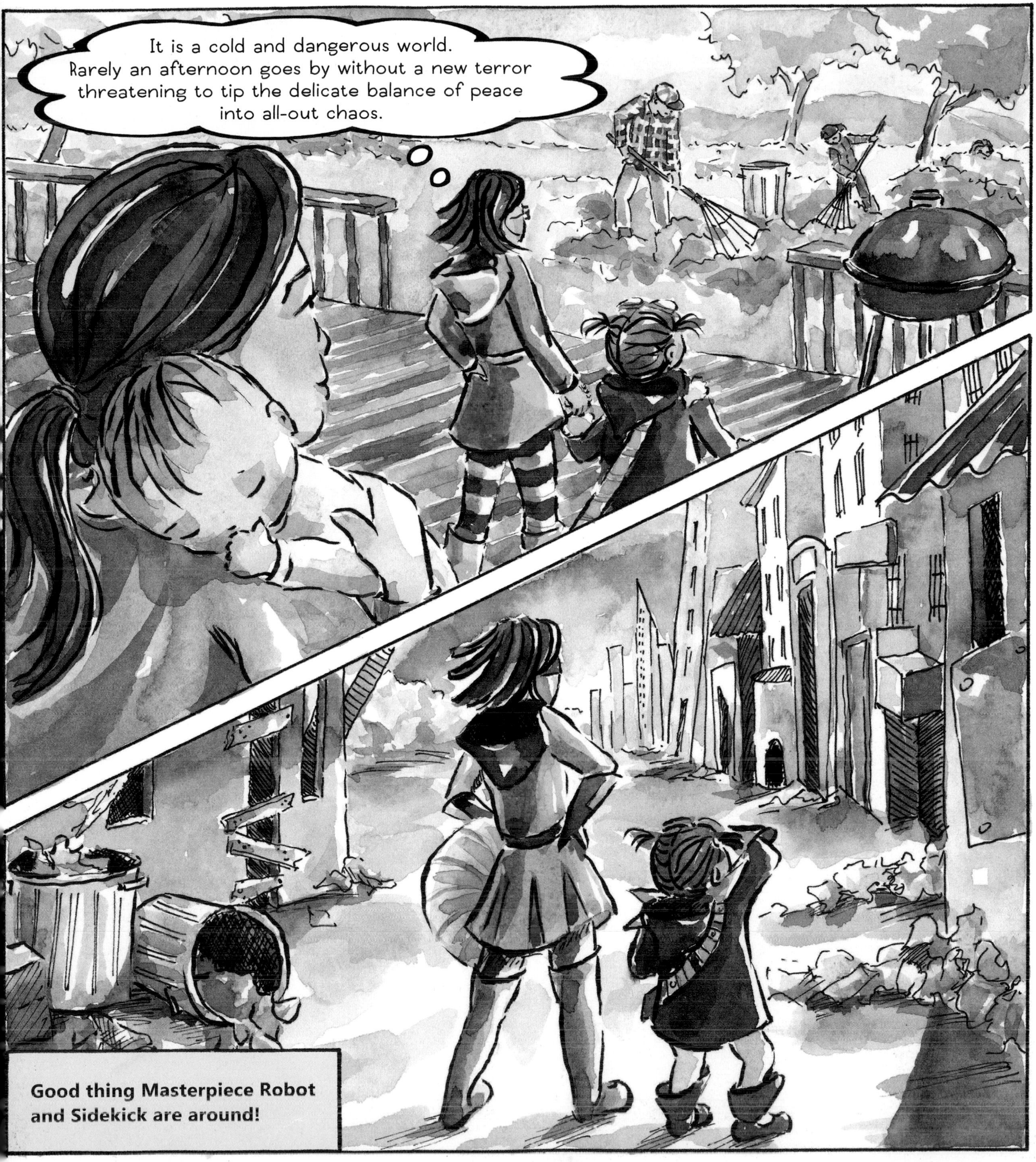
It is a cold and dangerous world. Rarely an afternoon goes by without a new terror threatening to tip the delicate balance of peace into all-out chaos.
Good thing Masterpiece Robot and Sidekick are around!

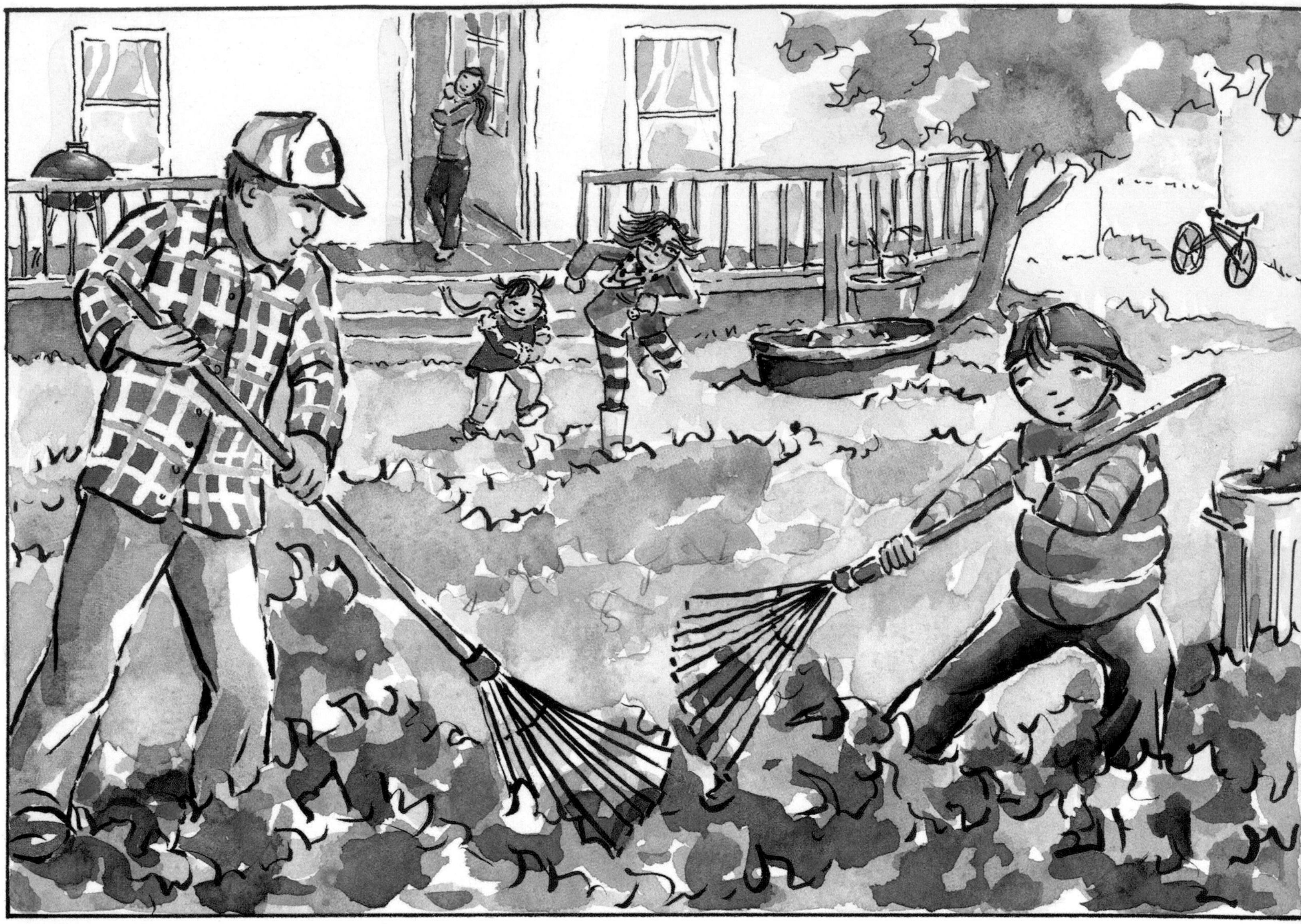

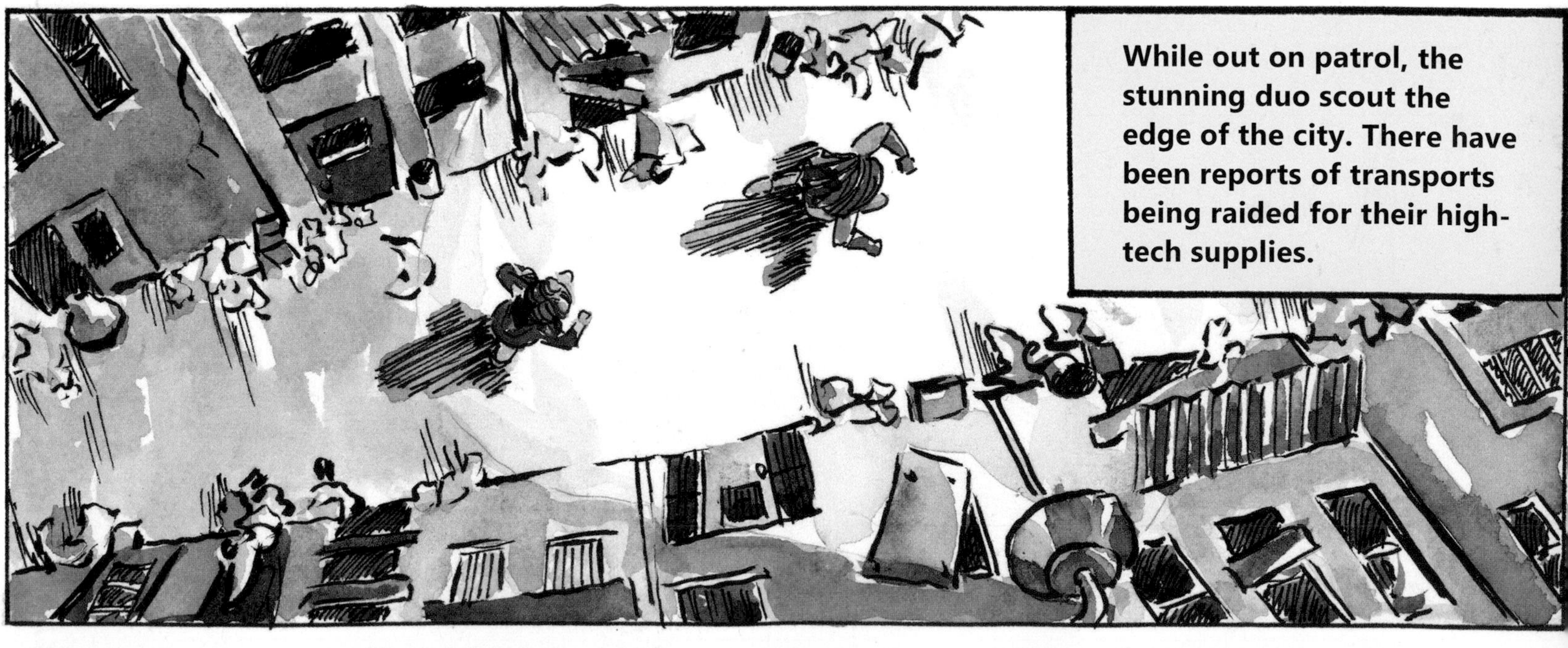
While out on patrol, the stunning duo scout the edge of the city. There have been reports of transports being raided for their high-tech supplies.

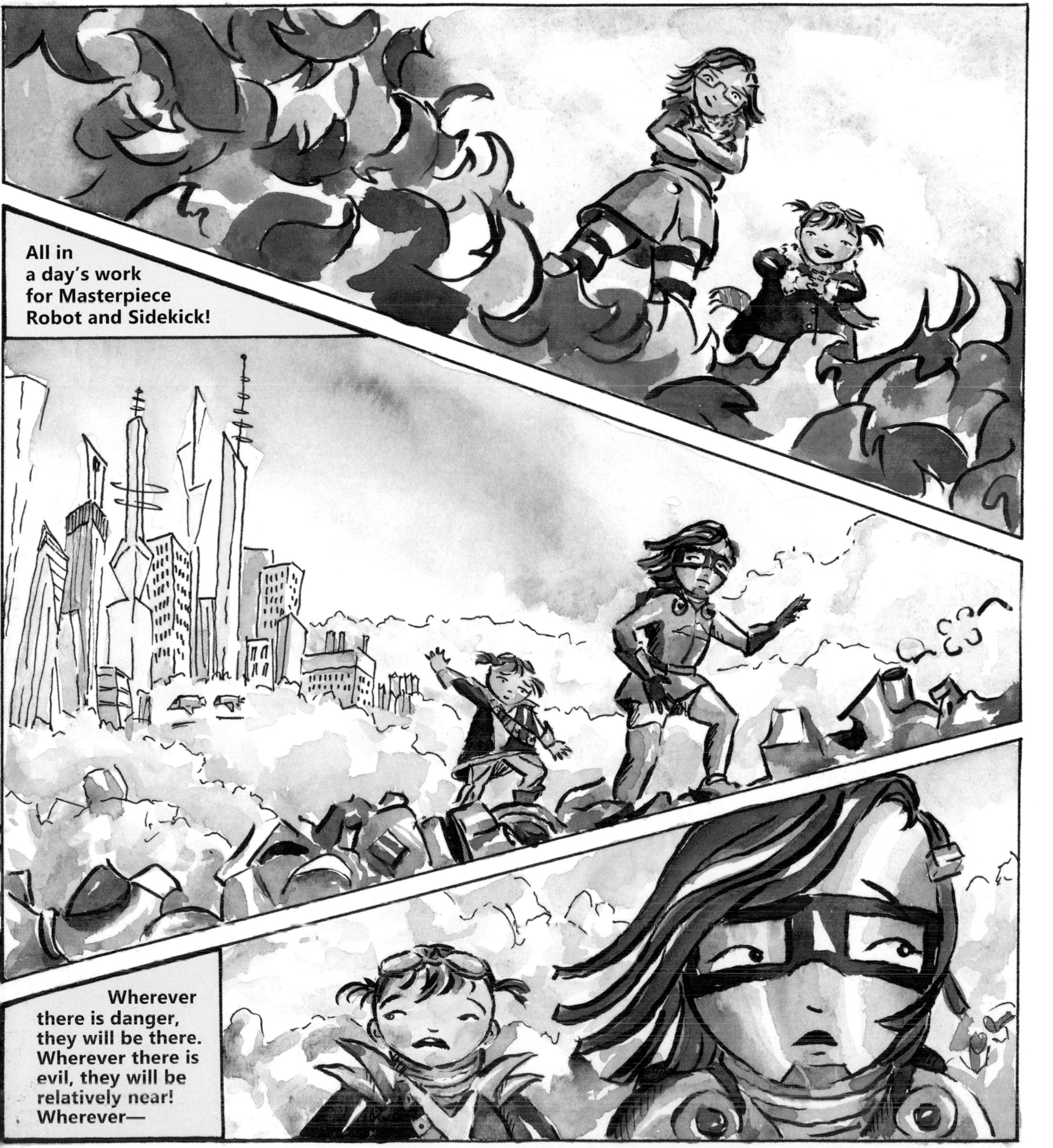
All in a day's work for Masterpiece Robot and Sidekick!
Wherever there is danger, they will be there. Wherever there is evil, they will be relatively near! Wherever—

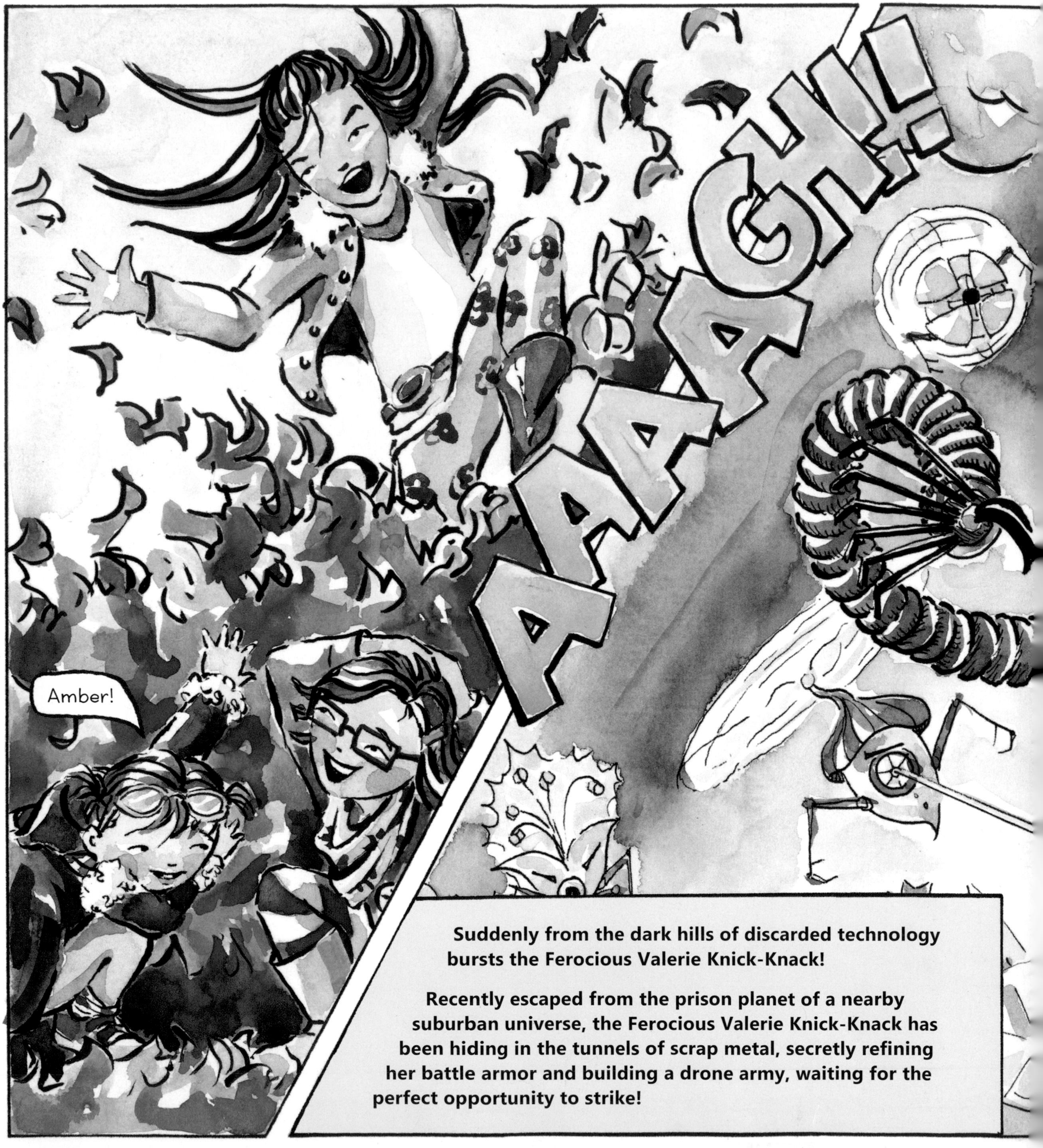
AAAAGH!!!
Amber!
Suddenly from the dark hills of discarded technology bursts the Ferocious Valerie Knick-Knack!
Recently escaped from the prison planet of a nearby suburban universe, the Ferocious Valerie Knick-Knack has been hiding in the tunnels of scrap metal, secretly refining her battle armor and building a drone army, waiting for the perfect opportunity to strike!

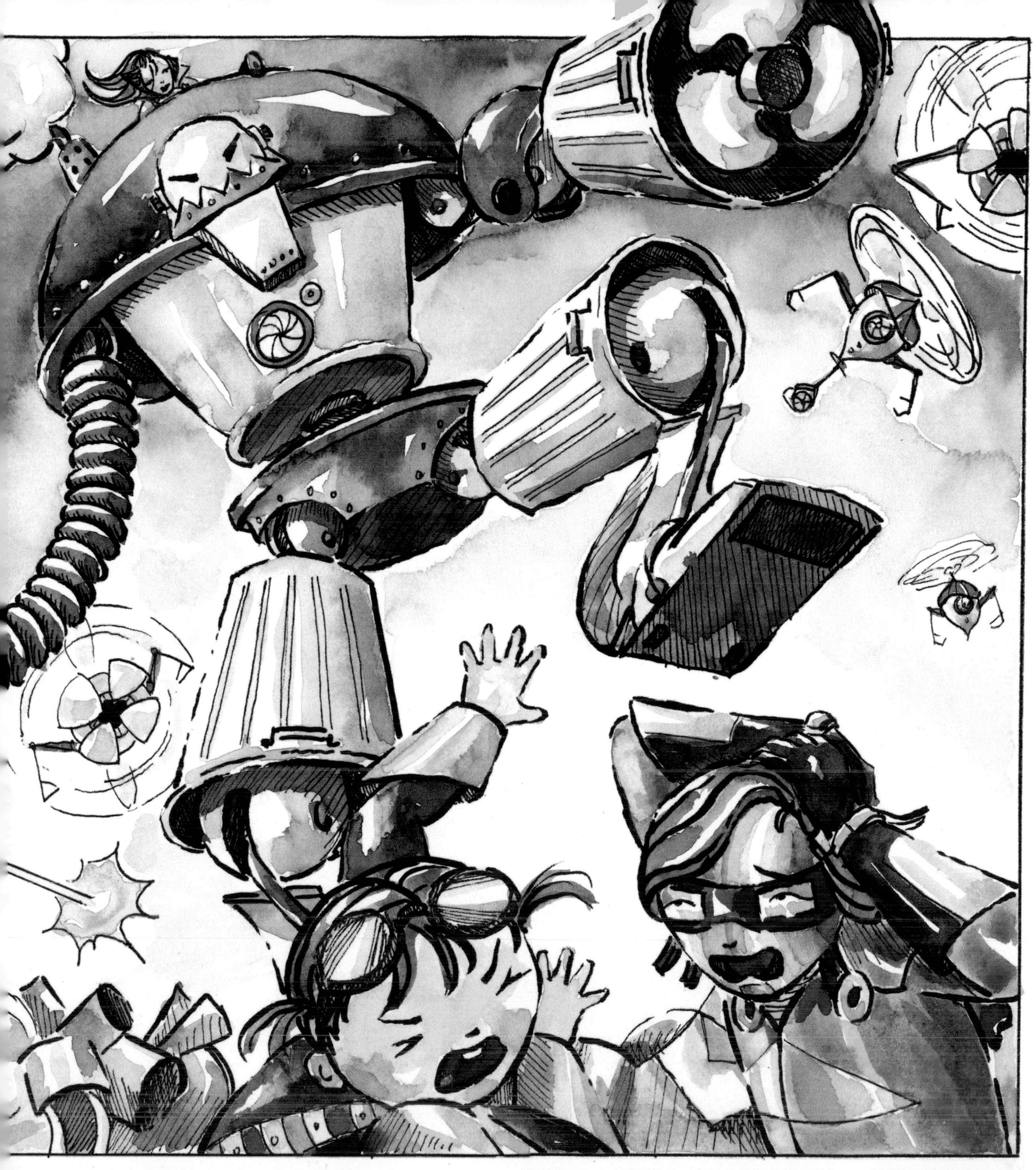

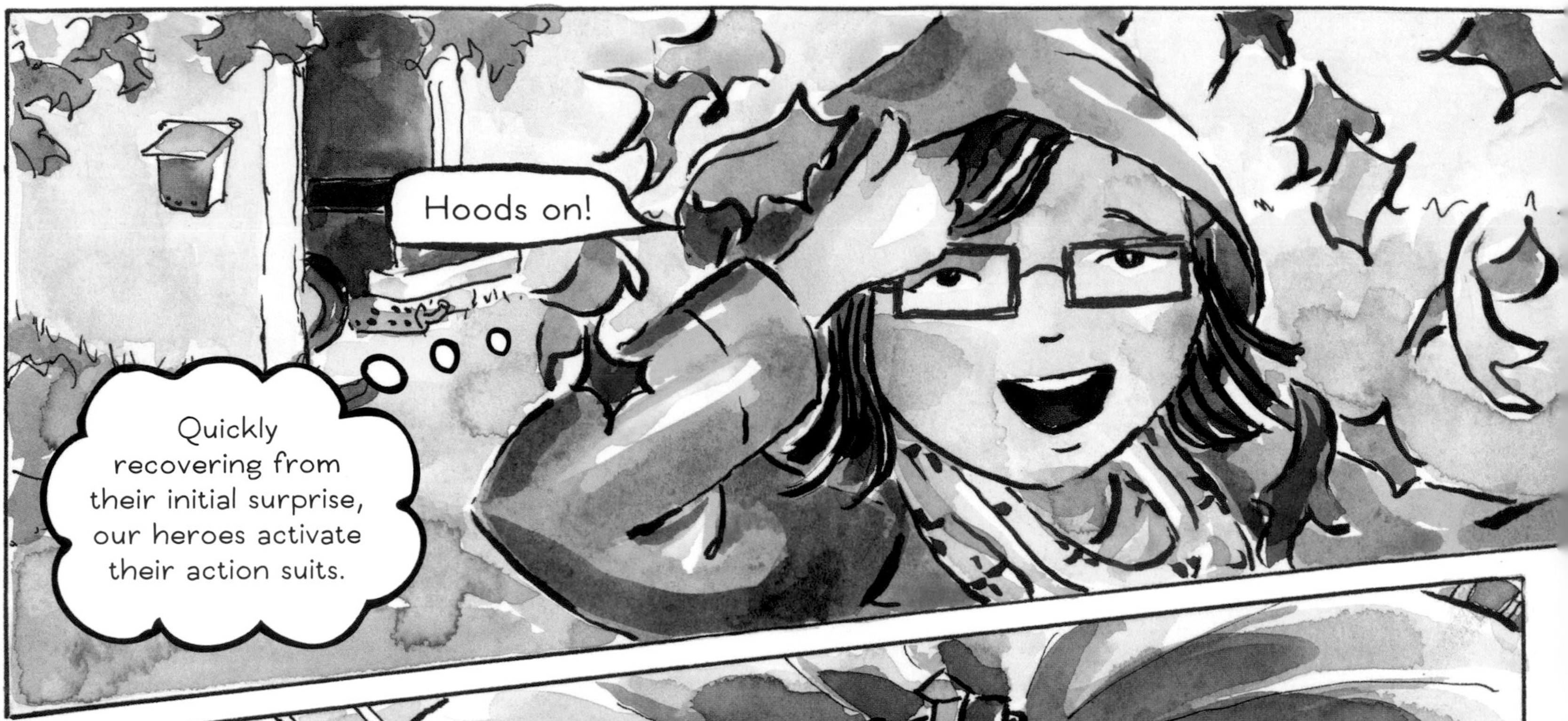
Hoods on!
Quickly recovering from their initial surprise, our heroes activate their action suits.

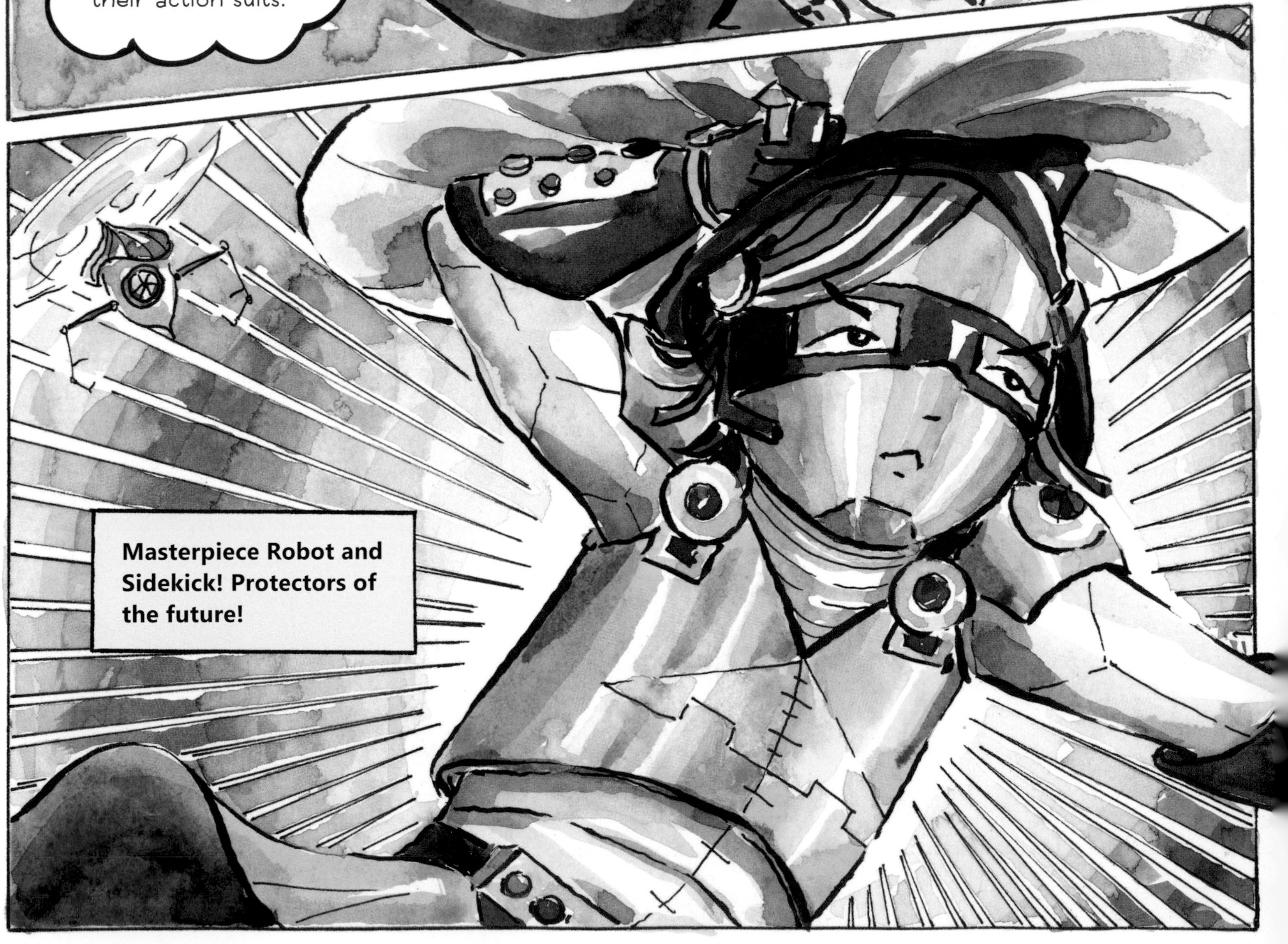
Masterpiece Robot and Sidekick! Protectors of the future!

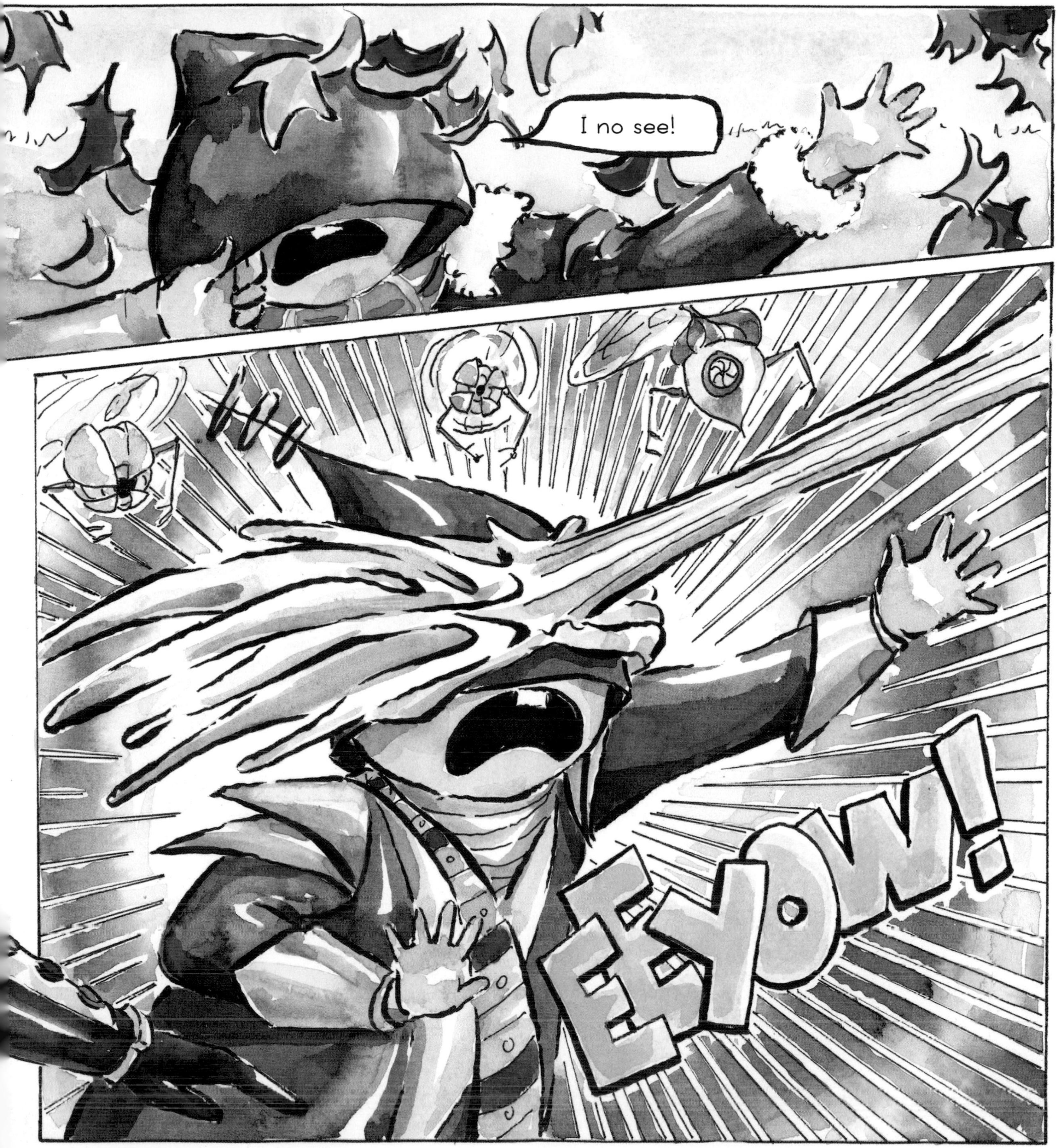
I no see!
EIYOW!

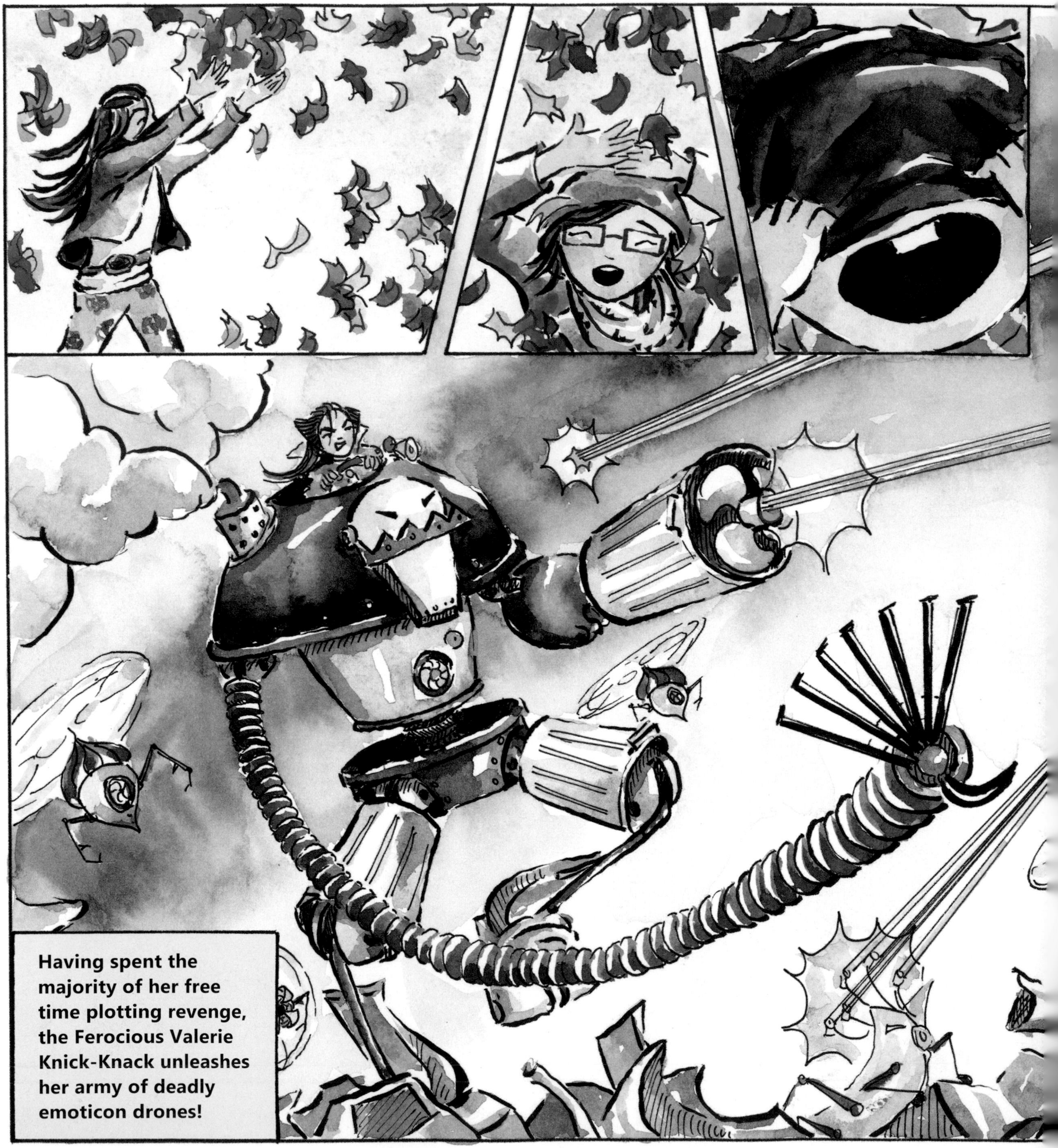
Having spent the majority of her free time plotting revenge, the Ferocious Valerie Knick-Knack unleashes her army of deadly emoticon drones!

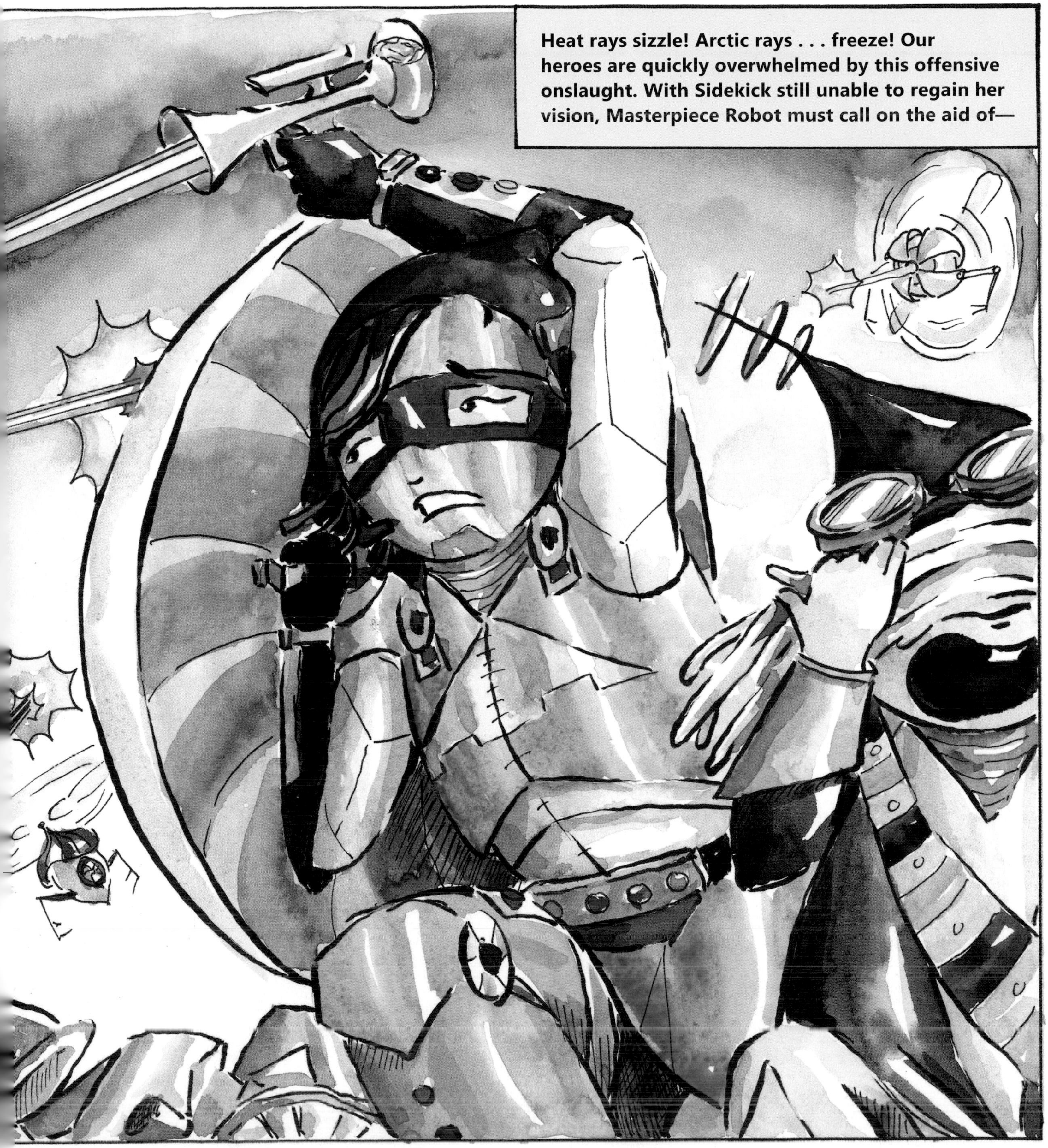
Heat rays sizzle! Arctic rays . . . freeze! Our heroes are quickly overwhelmed by this offensive onslaught. With Sidekick still unable to regain her vision, Masterpiece Robot must call on the aid of—

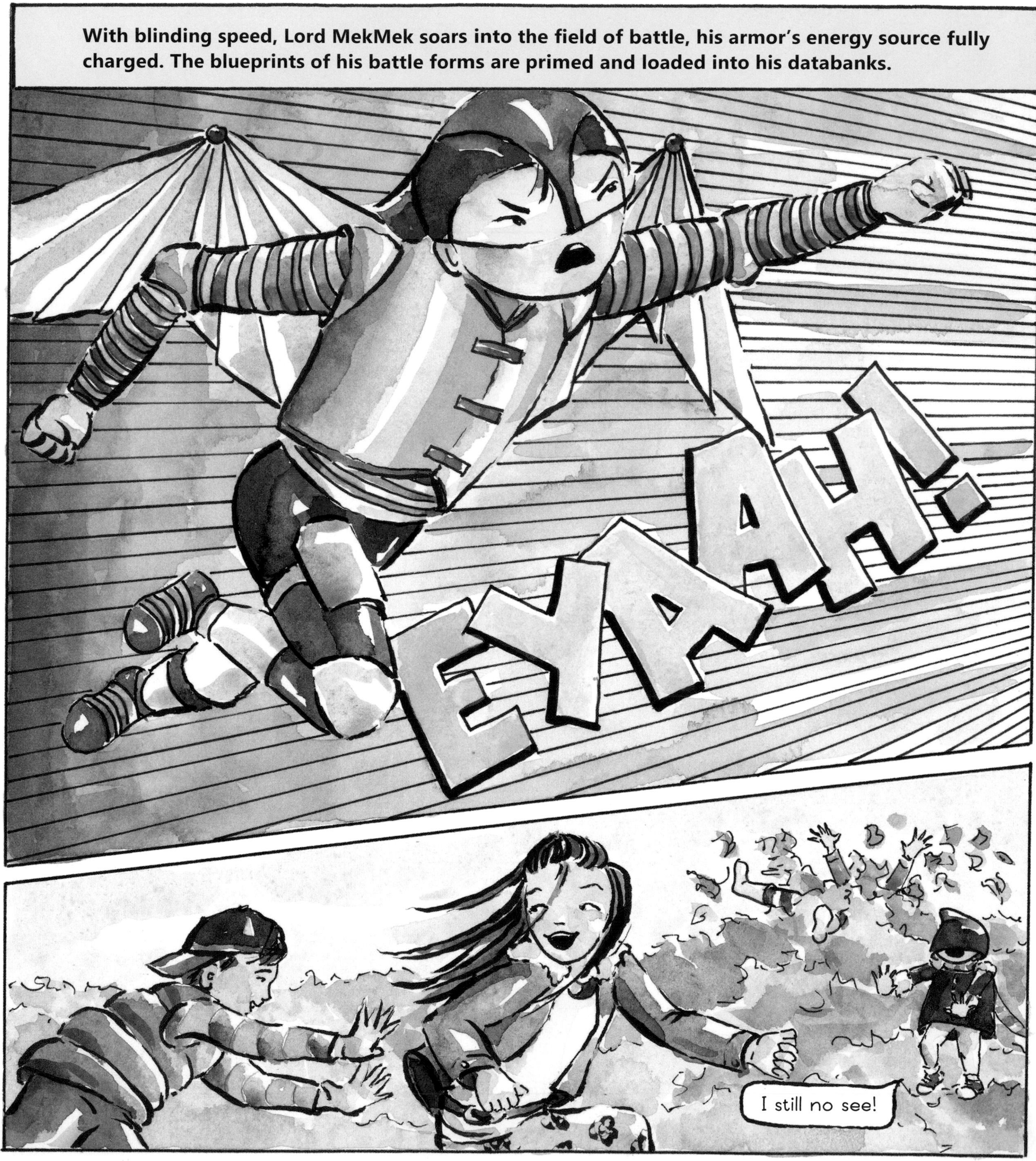
With blinding speed, Lord MekMek soars into the field of battle, his armor's energy source fully charged. The blueprints of his battle forms are primed and loaded into his databanks.
EYAAH!
I still no see!

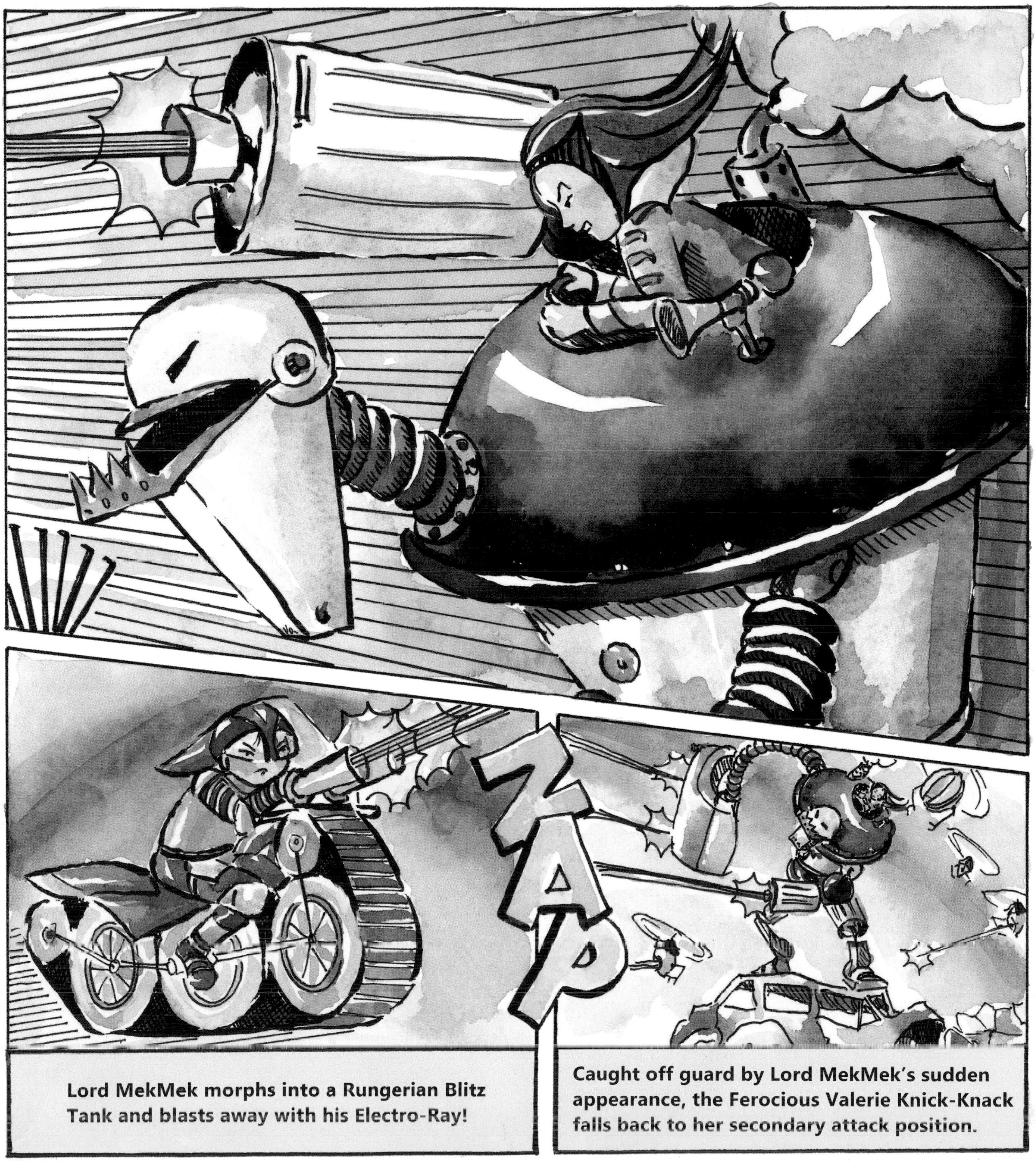
Lord MekMek morphs into a Rungerian Blitz Tank and blasts away with his Electro-Ray!
ZAP
Caught off guard by Lord MekMek's sudden appearance, the Ferocious Valerie Knick-Knack falls back to her secondary attack position.

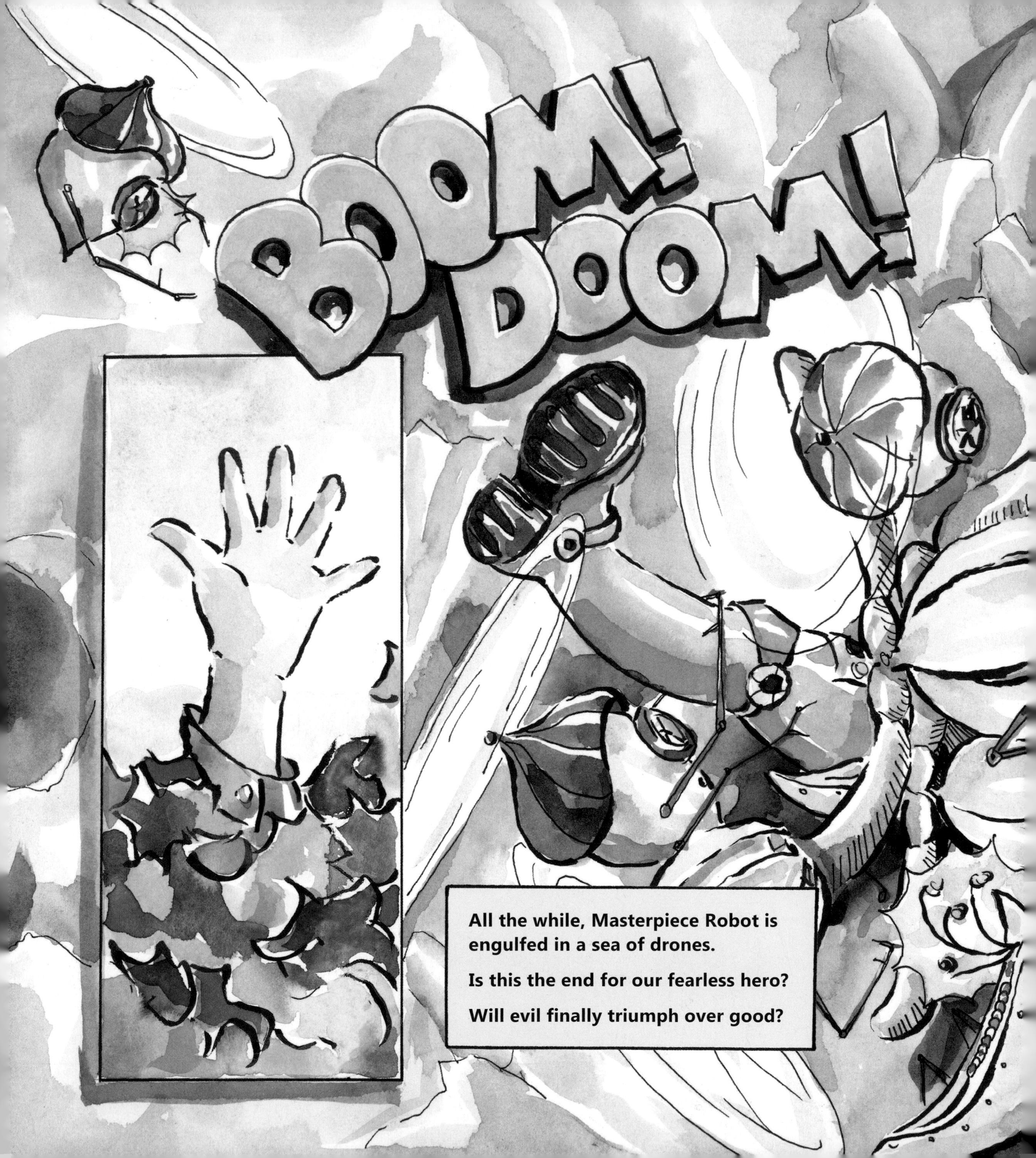
BOOM! DOOM!
All the while, Masterpiece Robot is engulfed in a sea of drones.
Is this the end for our fearless hero?
Will evil finally triumph over good?

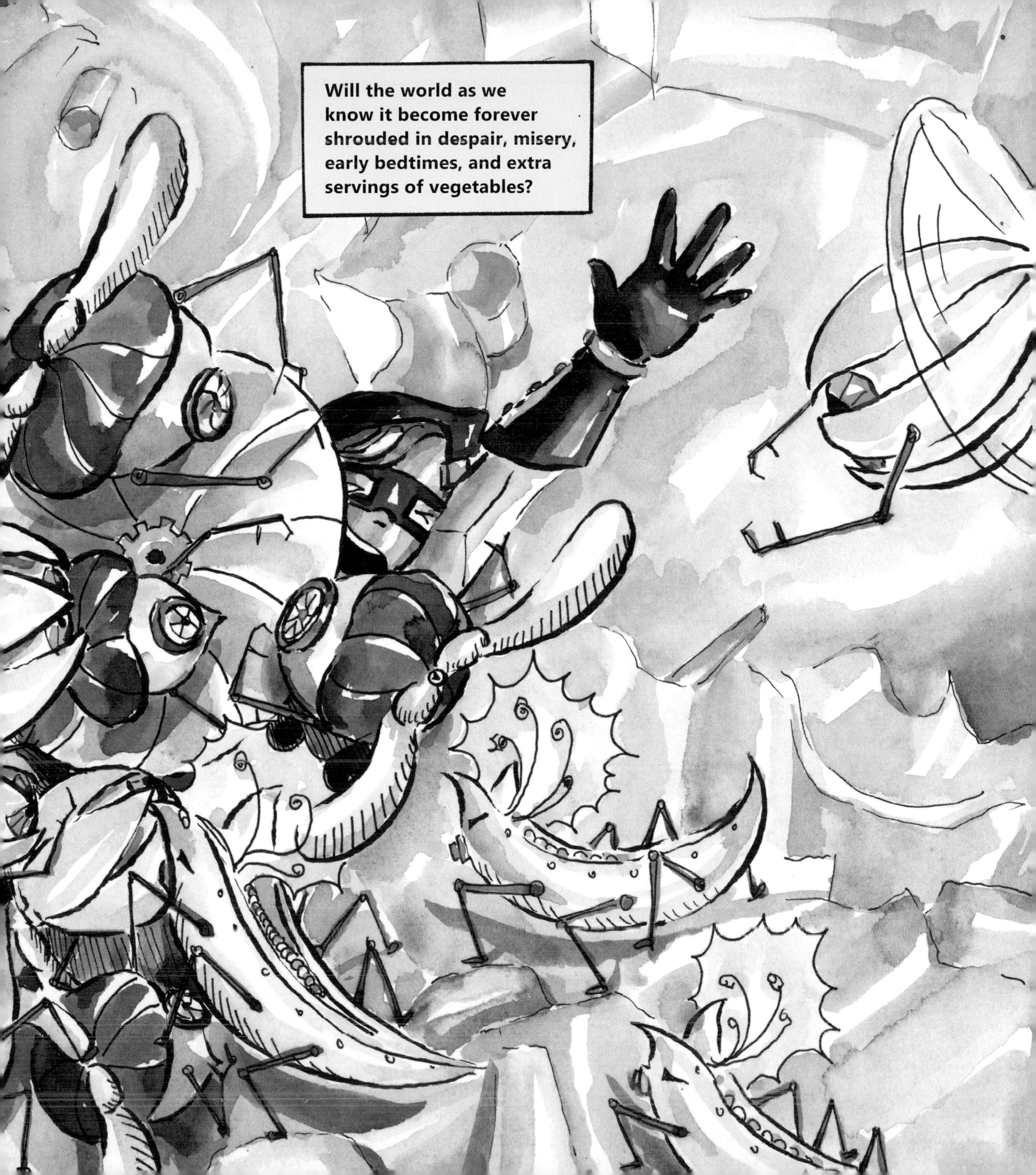
Will the world as we know it become forever shrouded in despair, misery, early bedtimes, and extra servings of vegetables?

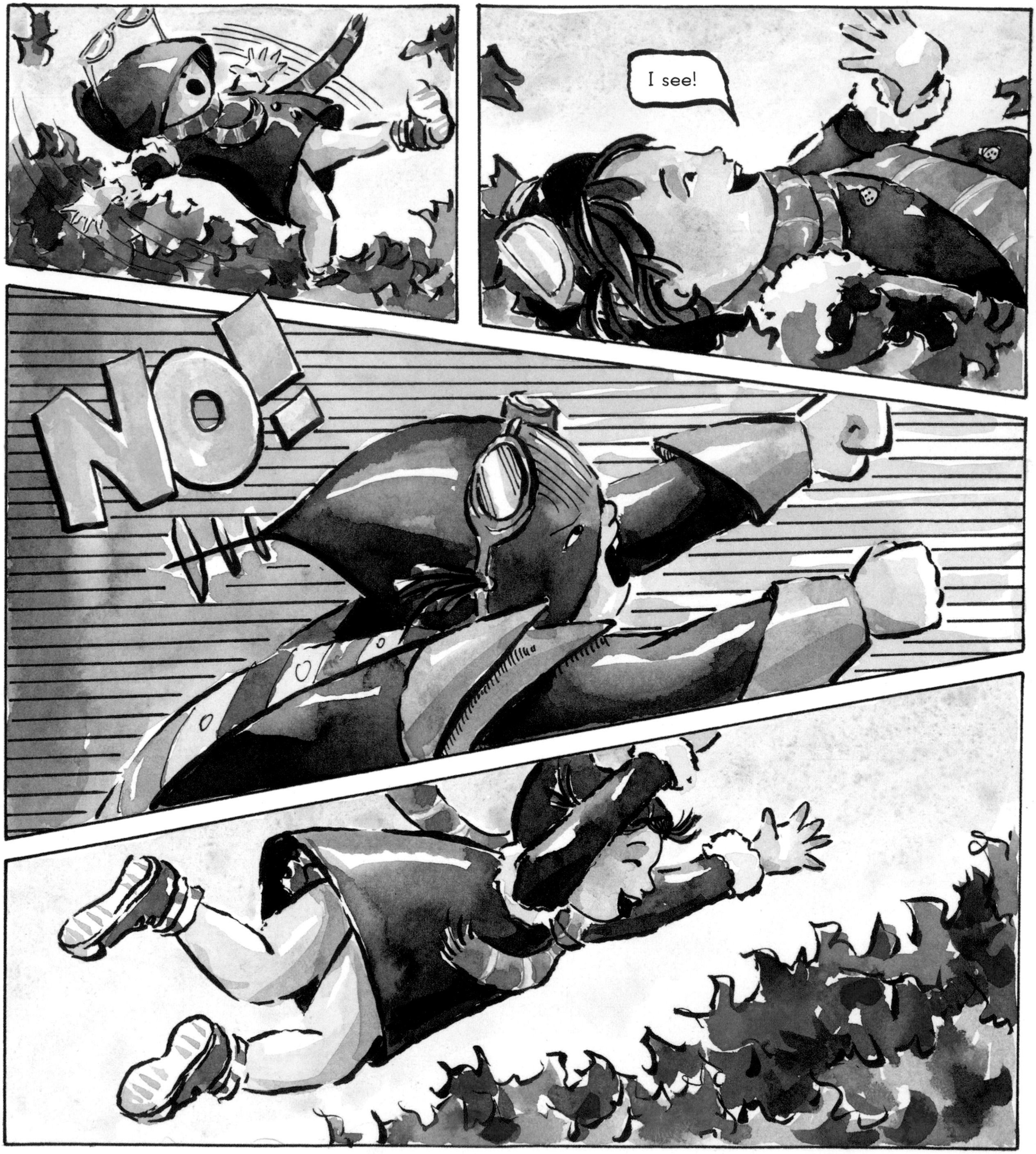
I see!
NO!

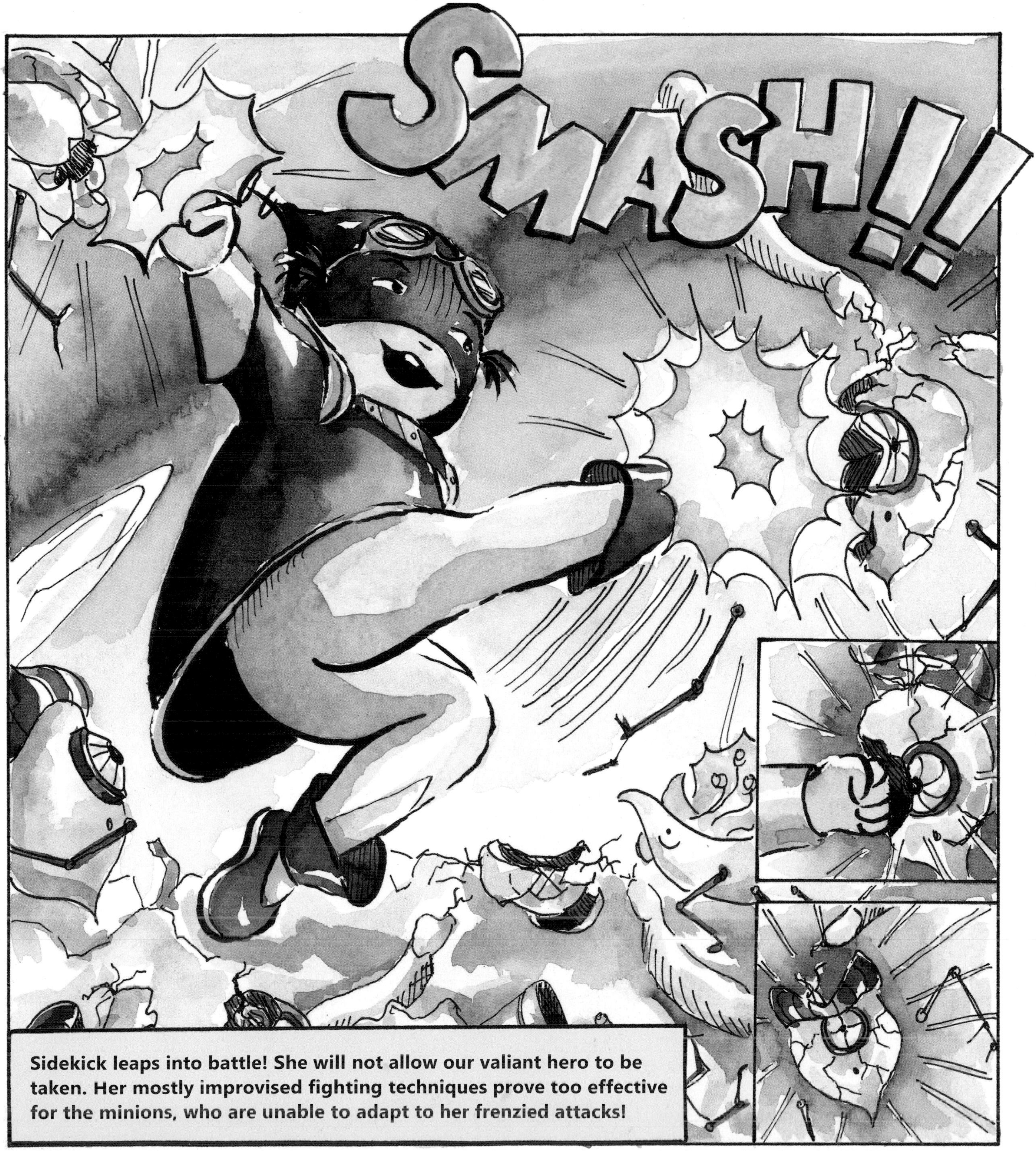
SMASH!!
Sidekick leaps into battle! She will not allow our valiant hero to be taken. Her mostly improvised fighting techniques prove too effective for the minions, who are unable to adapt to her frenzied attacks!

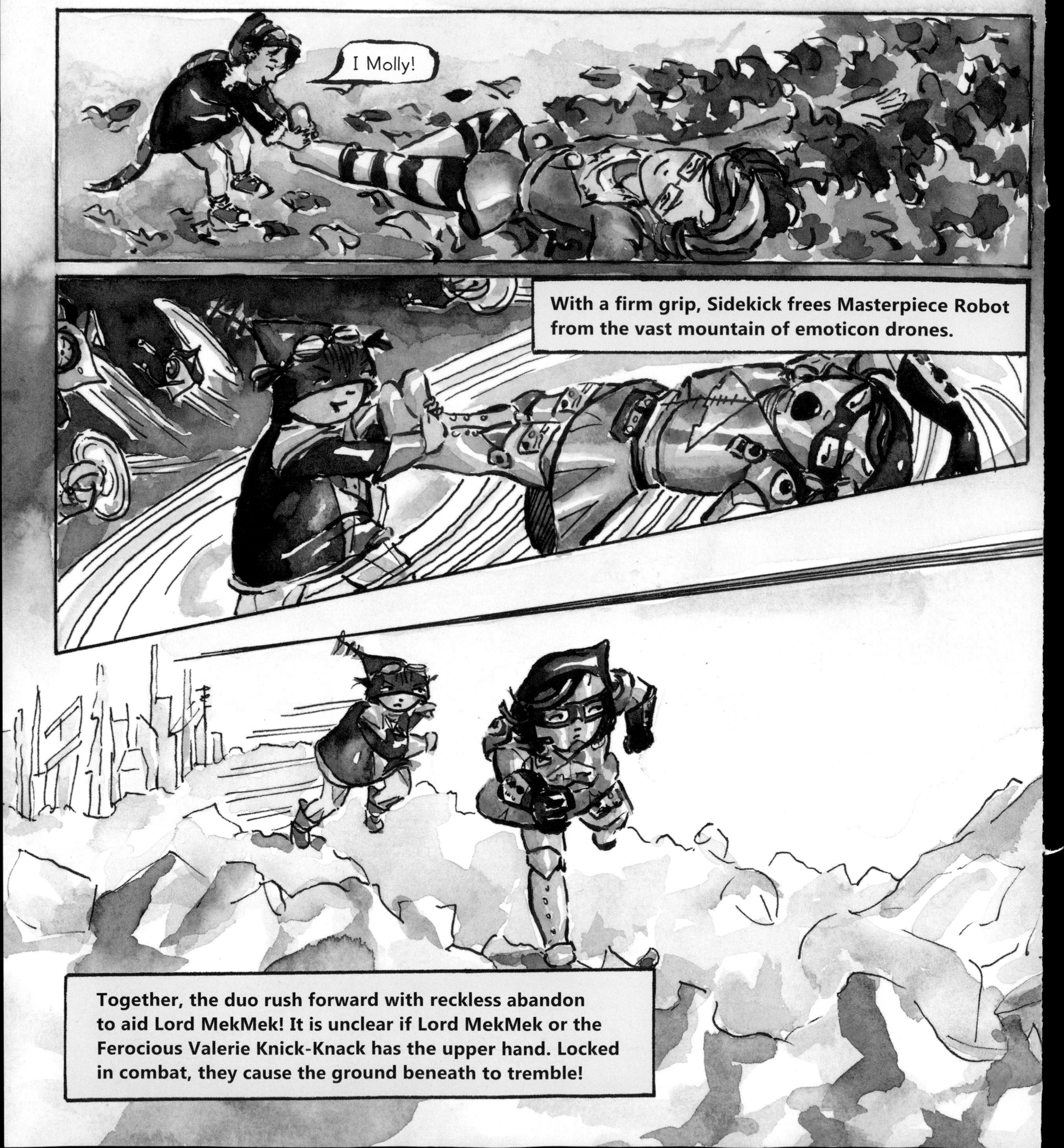
I Molly!
With a firm grip, Sidekick frees Masterpiece Robot from the vast mountain of emoticon drones.
Together, the duo rush forward with reckless abandon to aid Lord MekMek! It is unclear if Lord MekMek or the Ferocious Valerie Knick-Knack has the upper hand. Locked in combat, they cause the ground beneath to tremble!

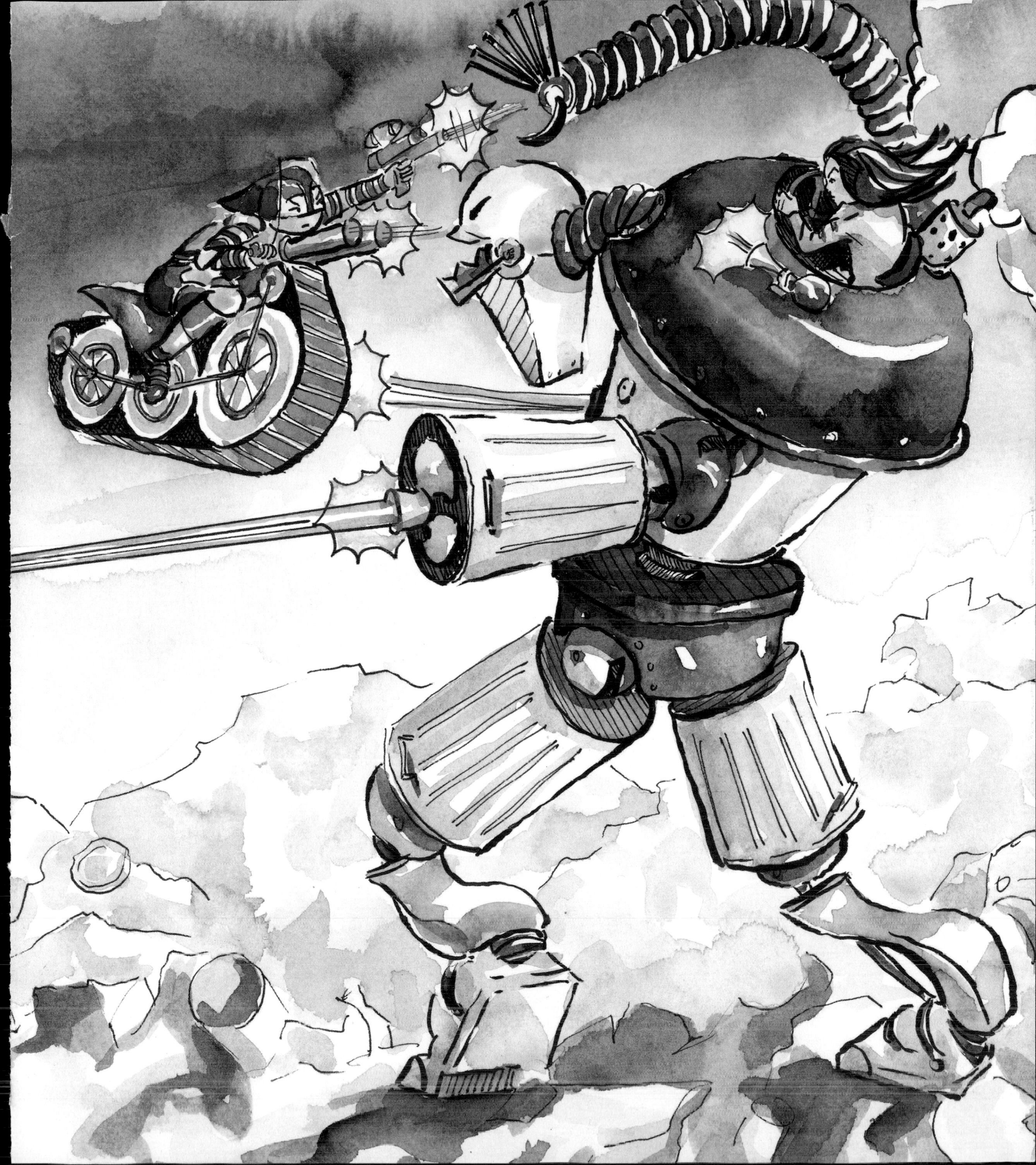

Surely Lord MekMek must soon succumb to the sheer fire-power of the Ferocious Valerie Knick-Knack. A titanic team-up may be the only way to defeat her and her drone army.

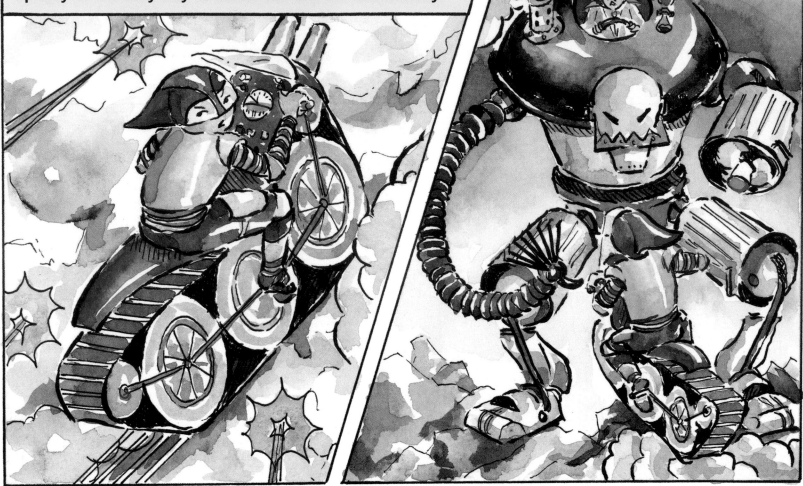

As night falls, Masterpiece Robot and Sidekick leap into the fray! The light is blinding as electricity fires one way and freezing rays go the other. Energy and plasma crackle in the night sky.

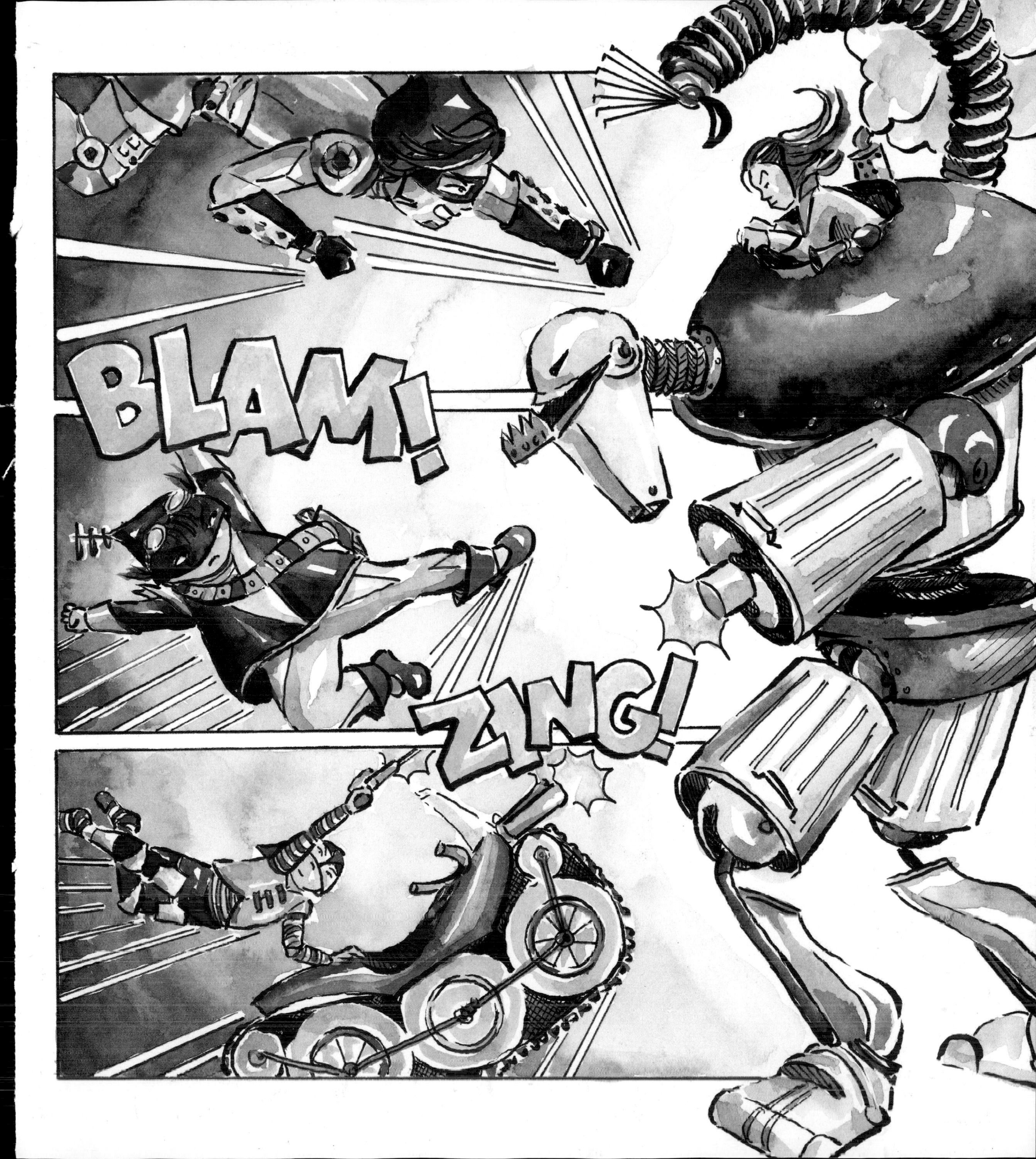
BLAM!
ZING!

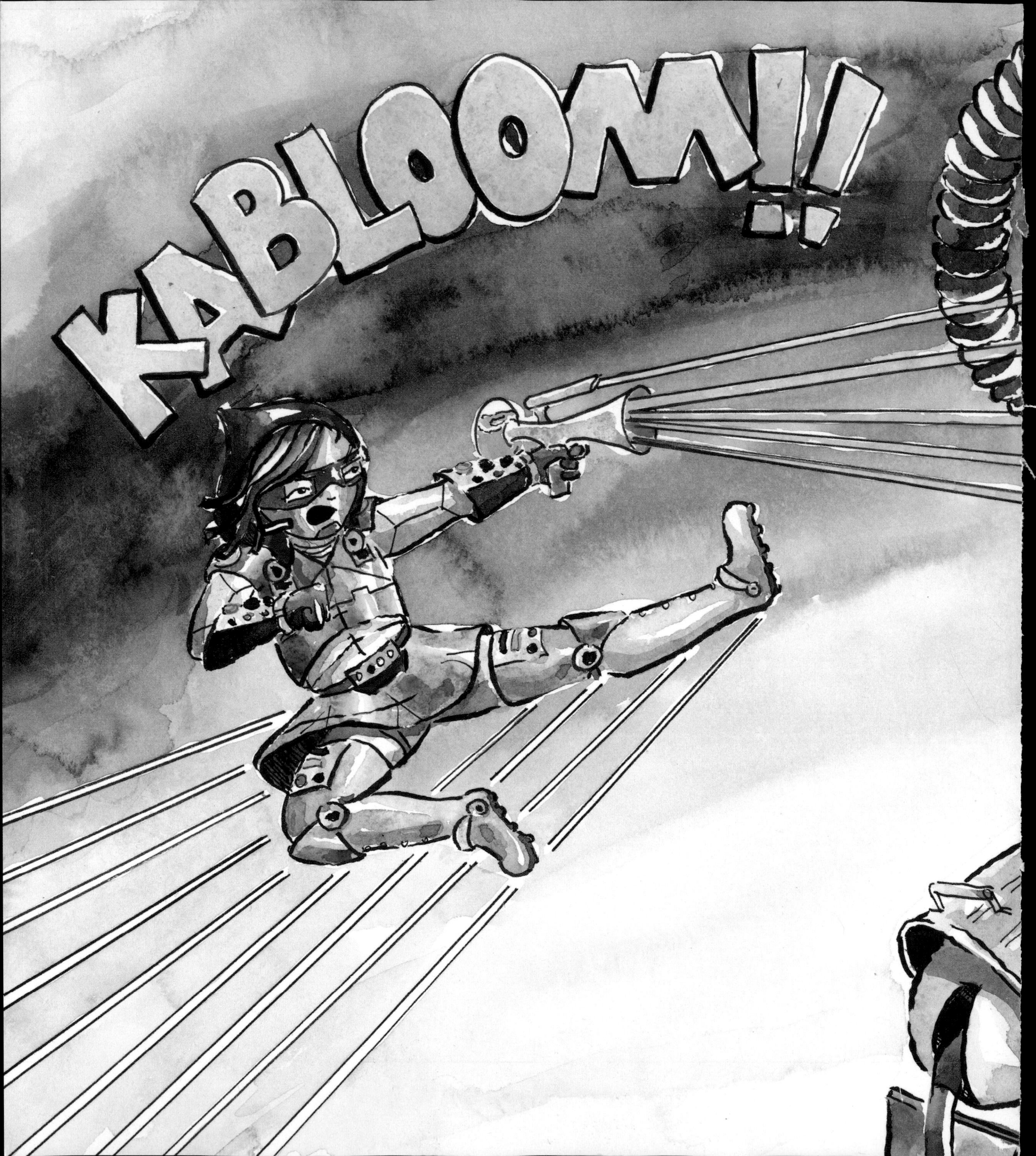
KABLOOM!!

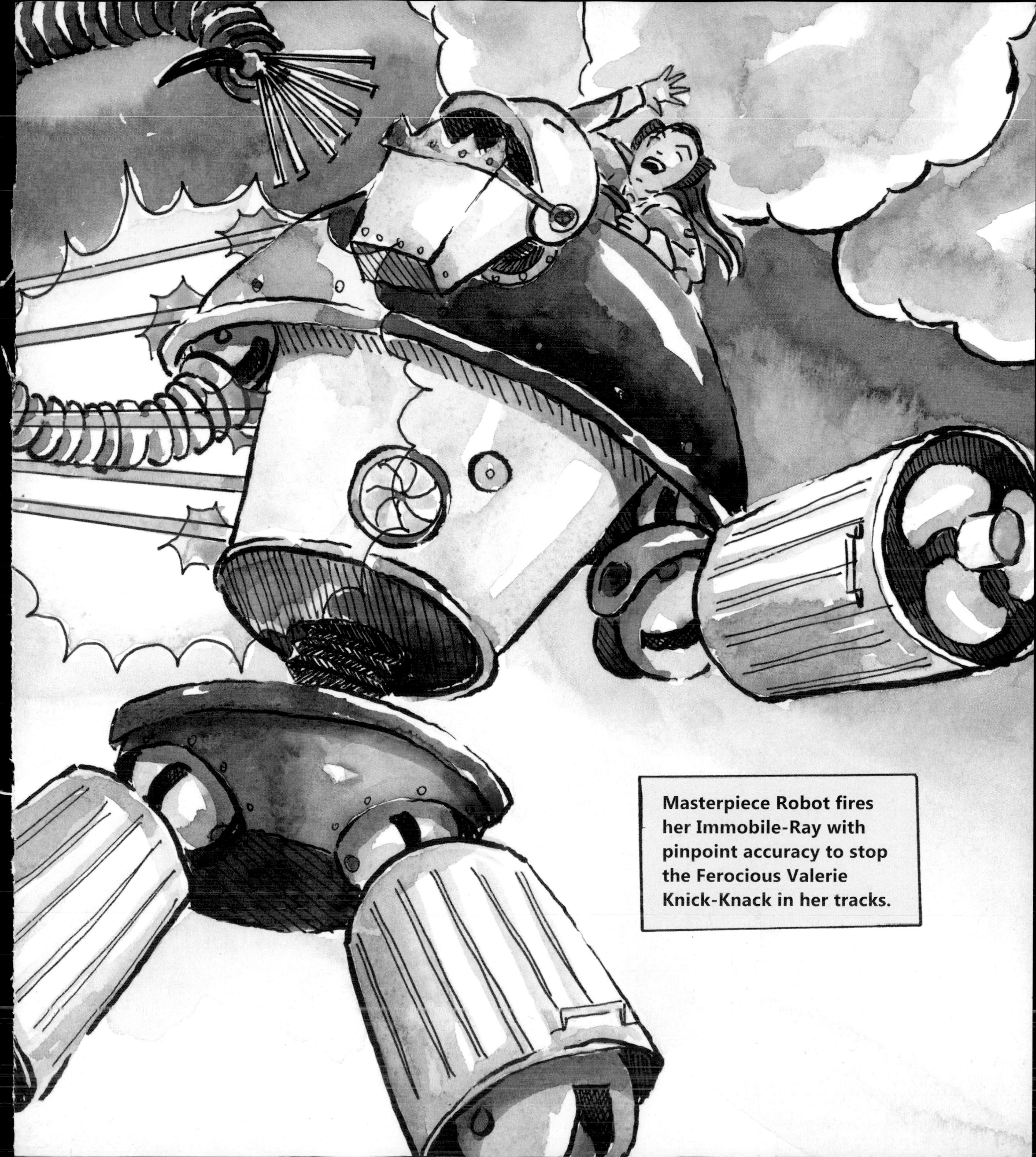
Masterpiece Robot fires her Immobile-Ray with pinpoint accuracy to stop the Ferocious Valerie Knick-Knack in her tracks.

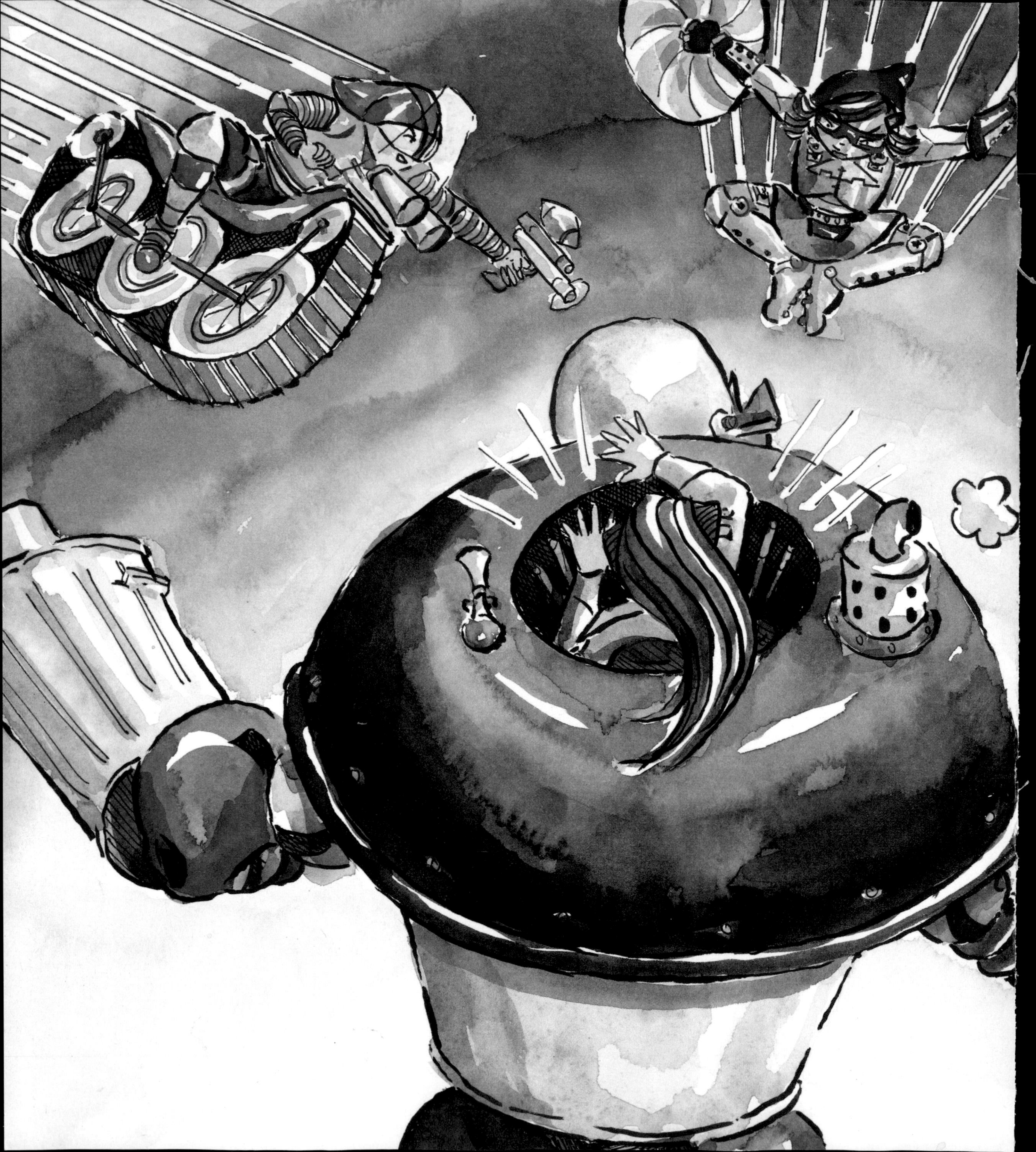

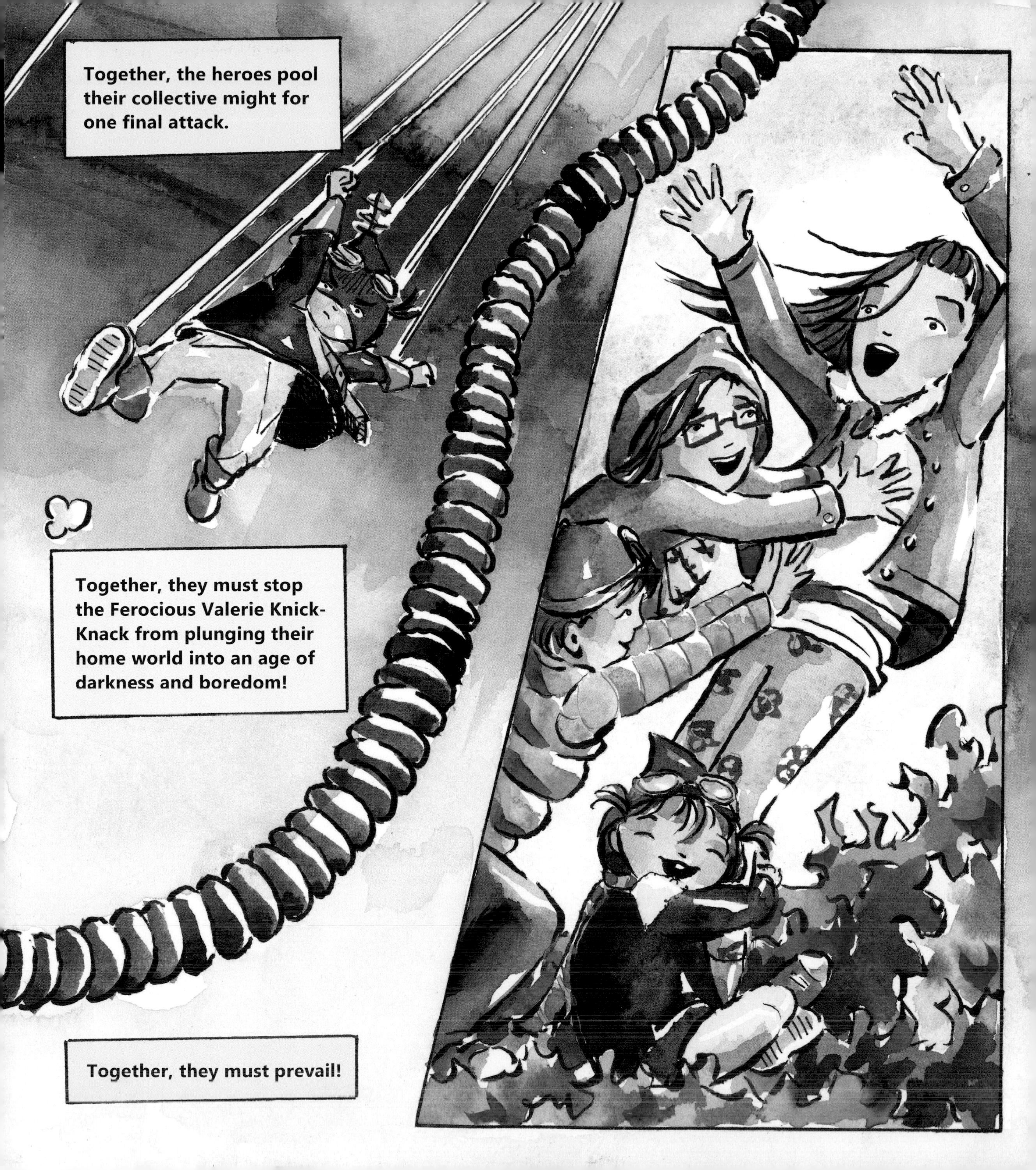
Together, the heroes pool their collective might for one final attack.
Together, they must stop the Ferocious Valerie Knick-Knack from plunging their home world into an age of darkness and boredom!
Together, they must prevail!

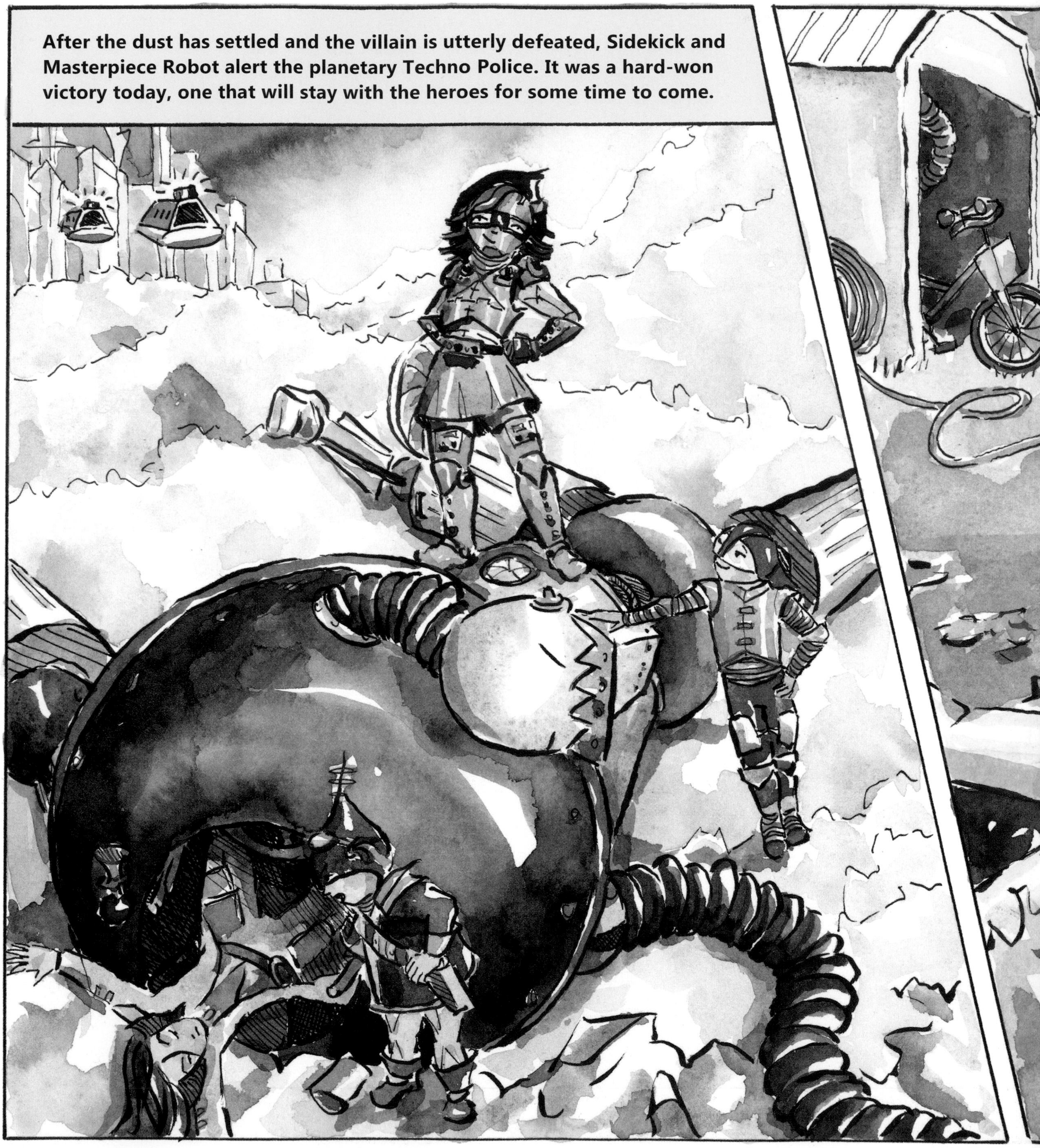
After the dust has settled and the villain is utterly defeated, Sidekick and Masterpiece Robot alert the planetary Techno Police. It was a hard-won victory today, one that will stay with the heroes for some time to come.

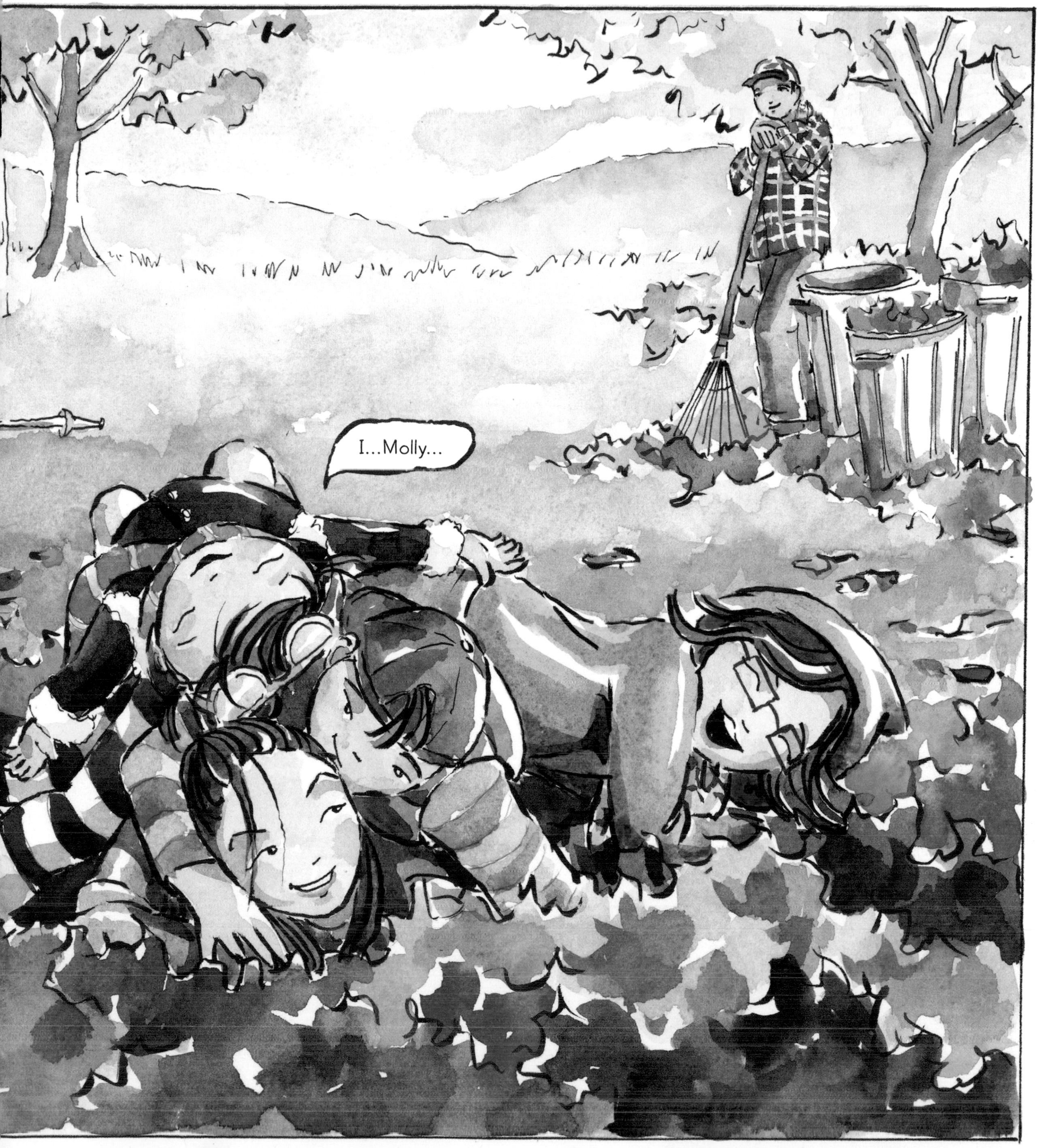
I...Molly...

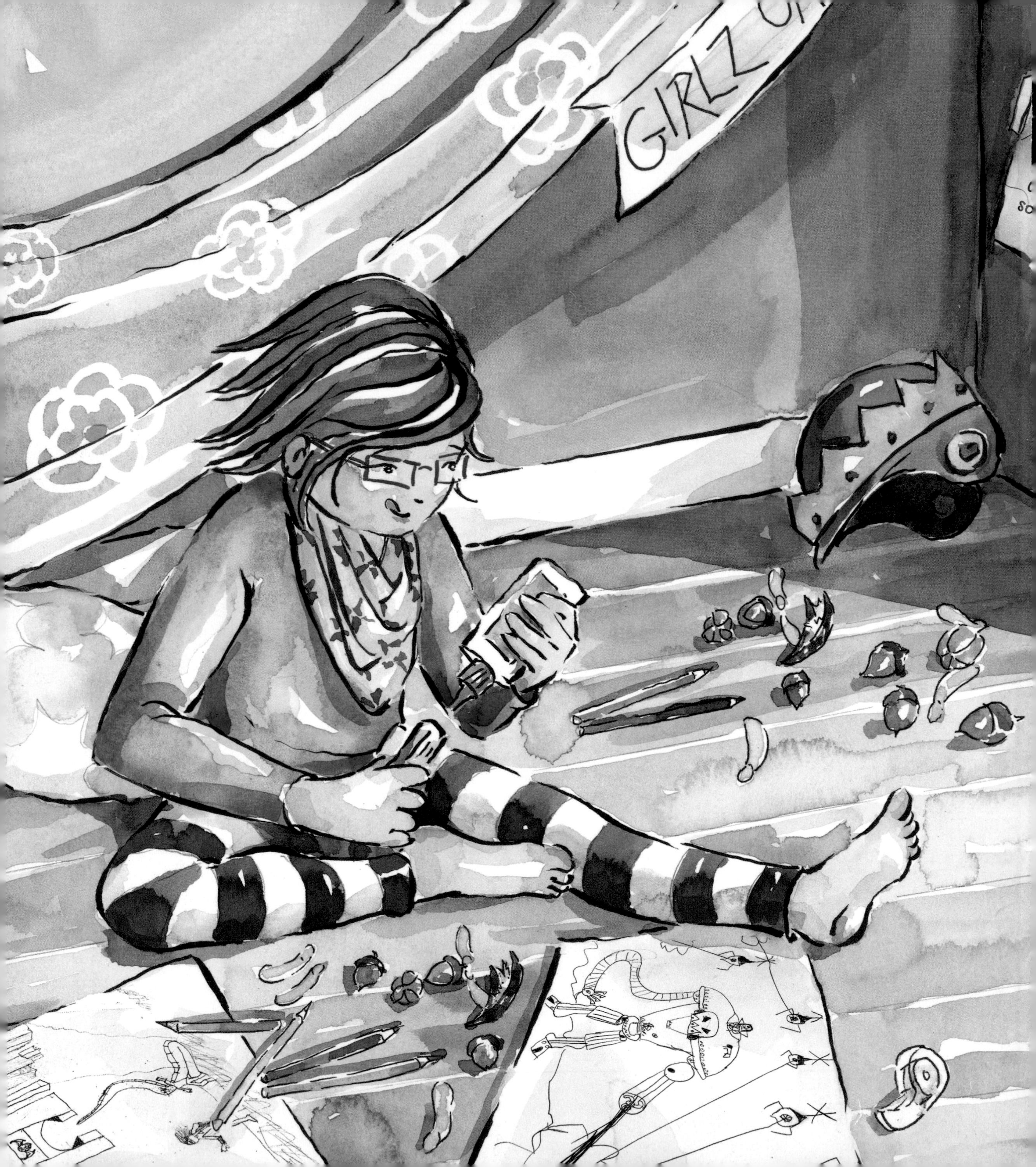
GIRLZ

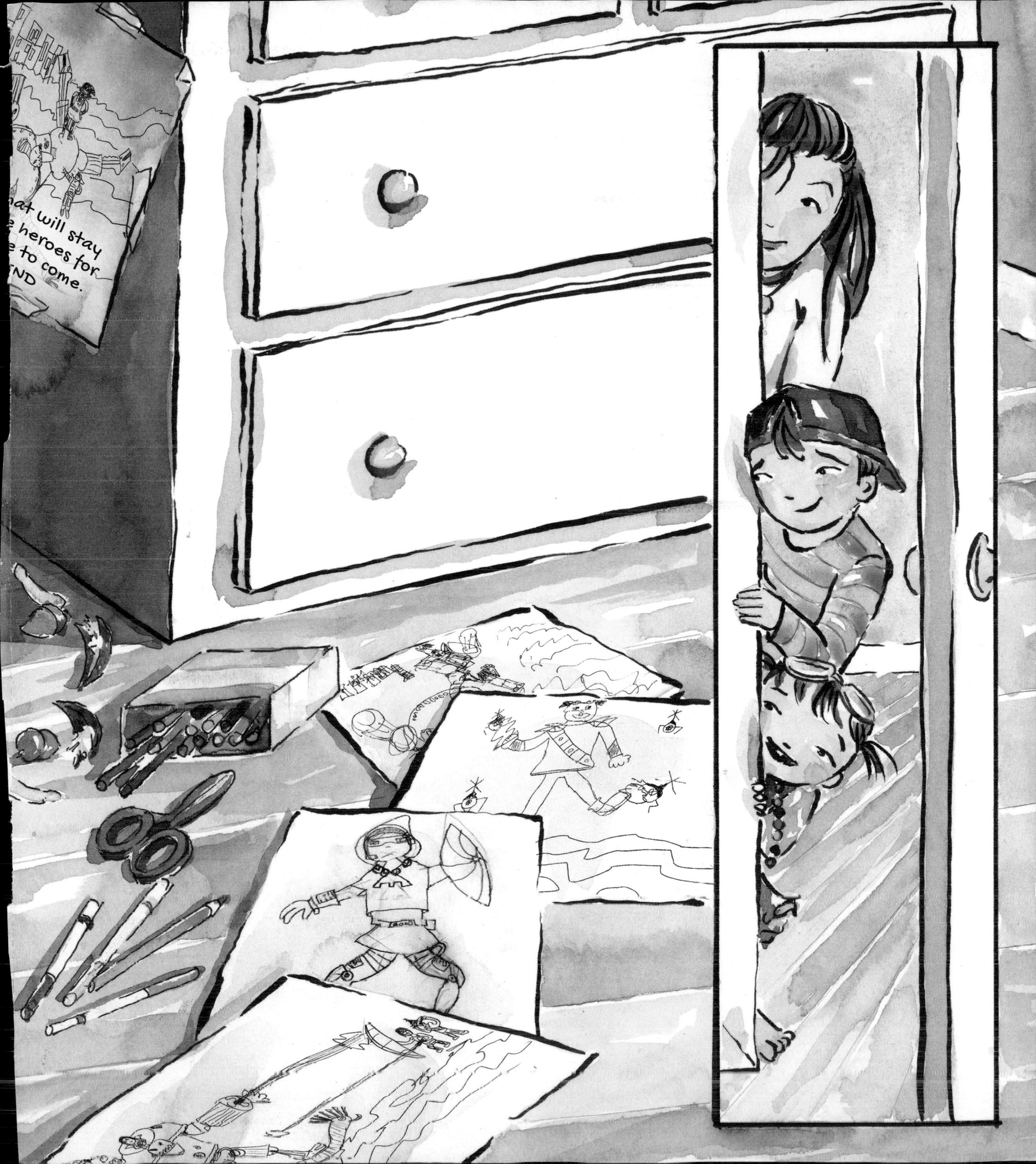
hat will stay
e heroes for
e to come.
ND

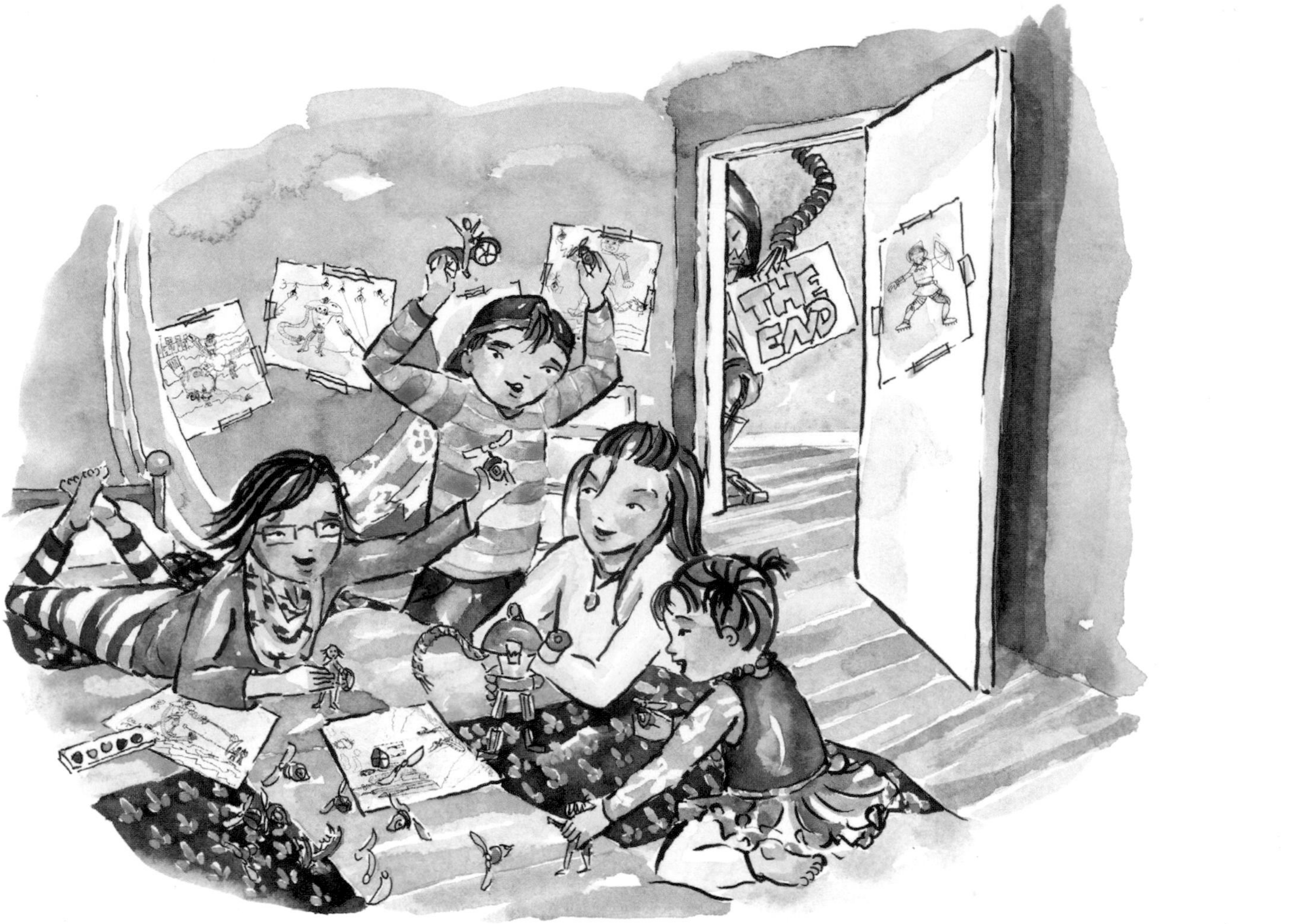
THE END

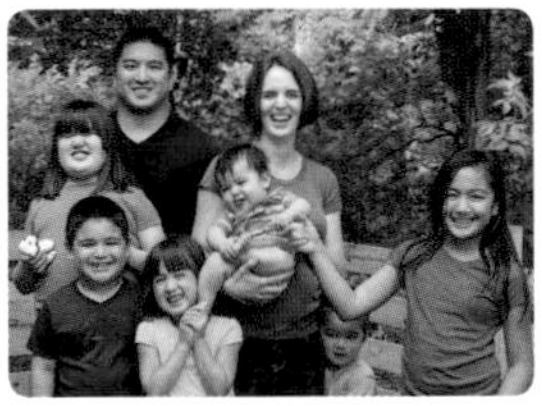

kschweitzerphoto.com

A child of Vietnamese immigrants, FRANK TRA proudly calls Wichita, Kansas, home. Frank attended the University of Kansas to wrestle and write comic books. While there, he also earned a Doctorate in Pharmacy. He has been a cancer pharmacist for the last ten years. Frank's writing credits include two graphic novels and several comic books. *Masterpiece Robot* is his first children's book. Dr. Tra resides in a quiet neighborhood with his wife, Katy, and their six children: Amber, Laura, Roman, Molly, Tommy, and Isaac. He spends his spare time writing, fishing, and coaching his high school wrestling team.

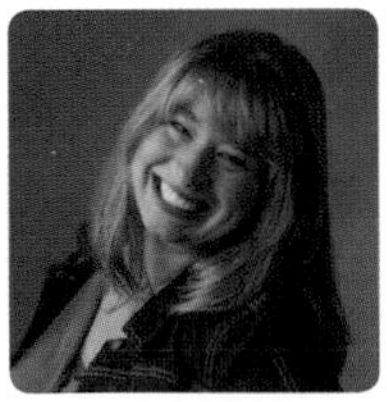

REBECCA EVANS worked for nine years as an artist and designer before returning to her first love: children's book illustration and writing. Her children's books include *Someday I'll Fly; Friends in Fur Coats; The Good Things; The Shopkeeper's Bear; Naughty Nana; Amhale in South Africa; Vivienne in France; Mei Ling in China; Marcela in Argentina; Tiffany in New York*; and *Tatiana in Russia*. She lives in Maryland with her husband and four young children, shares her love of literature and art regularly at elementary schools, teaches art at the Chesapeake Center for the Creative Arts, and works from her home studio whenever time permits. Rebecca's boundless imagination enjoys free rein at *www.rebeccaevans.net*.